"AH, ...ING
the finge... ... the
bowl of ... ...lol-
lop and ...

Neil ... ... her
hand to his lips instead. His g... ...cked
with hers, and he slowly drew her finger
into his mouth. When the chocolate was
gone, he licked her finger clean. "Very
tasty," he murmured. Slowly, like a cat, he
licked it again, though all traces of the
frosting had disappeared. "Very tasty."

Her knees buckled. She'd never known
that her finger was an erogenous zone, but
she felt heat stir low in her belly and
spread upward to warm her throat and
flush her cheeks. Alarmed by her reaction,
she jerked her finger away and averted her
gaze. "We still have to make the pastries
and clean up," she said quickly, and began
moving things around on the counter.

"Amy." Neil stilled her busy hands and
turned her shoulders toward him. "You
don't have to be afraid of me."

"Afraid? I'm not afraid of you. You just
make me nervous when you look at me
like that."

"And how do I look at you?"

"Like you'd like to eat me up."

"He smiled. "I would . . ."

WHAT ARE *LOVESWEPT* ROMANCES?

They are stories of true romance and touching emotion. We believe those two very important ingredients are constants in our highly sensual and very believable stories in the LOVESWEPT *line. Our goal is to give you, the reader, stories of consistently high quality that may sometimes make you laugh, sometimes make you cry, but are always fresh and creative and contain many delightful surprises within their pages.*

Most romance fans read an enormous number of books. Those they truly love, they keep. Others may be traded with friends and soon forgotten. We hope that each LOVESWEPT *romance will be a treasure—a "keeper." We will always try to publish*

LOVE STORIES YOU'LL NEVER FORGET BY AUTHORS YOU'LL ALWAYS REMEMBER

The Editors

Loveswept® 716

HOT
STREAK

JAN
HUDSON

BANTAM BOOKS
NEW YORK · TORONTO · LONDON · SYDNEY · AUCKLAND

HOT STREAK

A Bantam Book / November 1994

If you would be interested in receiving protective vinyl covers for your Loveswept books, please write to this address for information:

Loveswept
Bantam Books
P.O. Box 985
Hicksville, NY 11802

ISBN 0-553-44435-2

Published simultaneously in the United States and Canada

PRINTED IN THE UNITED STATES OF AMERICA

OPM   0 9 8 7 6 5 4 3 2 1

For all my friends with unusual gifts.

A special thanks to Paris Jhtabchi, owner of Croissant Brioche French Bakery and Café in Houston, for some of the finer points of bread making and brick ovens.

Thanks also to Mike Arnold, Chief of Security, and George Staresinic, Director of Advertising and Public Relations, at the Riviera Hotel and Casino in Las Vegas for their information, cordiality, and cooperation. These are good folks.

ONE

The pane squeaked as Amy Jordan wiped a little spot in the condensation to peek out the bakery window that fronted Jackson Square.

He was still there.

An extremely handsome man from what she could tell, he'd been sitting on that bench almost all day, staring into space, looking totally dejected and forlorn. Nicely dressed in a conservative suit and tie, he had a small suitcase at his feet and a raincoat folded atop the garment bag lying on the bench beside him.

He hadn't moved since she spotted him around noon, not even to don his raincoat when the damp, overcast day turned to drizzle, and it was now six-thirty and almost closing time. With the growing dusk and messy weather, the artists and street vendors had packed up and gone home for the day, and the nightlife was not yet in full swing. As crazy as the natives and tourists were, nobody else was sitting in the rain.

Amy had been curious about him earlier, but now she started to worry. Her sister Rachel, who owned the bakery, would have told her to blow it off and mind her own business. After all, Rachel always said, half the nut cases in the United States eventually made their way to New Orleans and Jackson Square—those who didn't stay in California. But Rachel was a cynic, and Amy didn't have a cynical bone in her body.

In fact Rachel—and a few other people she could name offhand—had accused her of being hopelessly naive and gullible enough to buy swamp land from every snake oil salesman that came down the pike. That wasn't true. One couldn't spend two years as a social worker in a children's hospital and four years in Dallas's inner city and remain naive. Burned-out, soul-shattered? Yes. Naive? No. Nor was she gullible. Not exactly. She was simply tenderhearted and a natural born nurturer. And if being so had gotten her into trouble a time or two . . . well, several times, that was a price she willingly paid for caring.

And she did care. Deeply. Excruciatingly.

That's why she dithered over the man on the bench.

His blond hair had darkened from the drizzle, and his clothes were getting soaked. Amy was sure that something must be seriously wrong. He might be ill. Or have amnesia and be lost. October's first cool front was sweeping through the city and bringing more rain. Of course it wasn't supposed to get below sixty degrees, but still, he could get pneumonia if he sat out there all night. She couldn't just let him stay there all alone in the rain, could she?

Certainly not.

She grabbed her umbrella from behind the counter, and the bell above the door tinkled as she went outside. Strains of a lonely blues song from Pop's Place drifted across the square and under the dripping canopy, the melancholy sax overlaying the sodden air with a bone-deep sadness that seemed to match the droop of the man's shoulders.

Unfurling the umbrella that looked liked a giant red poppy, she held it above her head and tiptoed through the shallow puddles. "Excuse me," she said, trying to get close enough to shelter him with the red petals and still respect his space. "Excuse me."

He turned his head slightly and glanced up at her with eyes that took her breath away. Blue as the shallows of the Caribbean, they seemed to draw her into depths that rivaled an ocean abyss. But something other than the beauty of his eyes struck her. Pain. Shock. Sorrow. She had seen enough of it, experienced enough of it to identify it. Gut-wrenching misery bled from his eyes, seeped from his pores, and slithered into her heart as if by osmosis. She had to consciously throw up barriers against his pain.

"May I help you in some way?" she asked.

He shook his head and looked away.

"How about a cup of coffee? You need to get out of this rain. It's going to get worse." She touched his shoulder. "You're going to catch cold."

"I don't give a damn," he mumbled.

"Now is that any way to talk? Of course you care. Or you will when you start coughing and going through a box of tissues a day. At least come inside the bakery for a minute and have a cup of coffee." She gave him her warmest smile and tugged on his coat sleeve.

He shrugged, stood, and started for the bakery, leaving his belongings behind. Holding the umbrella handle between her chin and shoulder, Amy quickly scooped up his things and hurried after him.

When he opened the door and noticed her struggling with his baggage, he mumbled,

"Sorry," then took his things and tossed them on the floor just inside the door.

"No problem." She smiled again, let down the umbrella and shook it, then bustled into the bakery that was fragrant with yeasty aromas and warm from the wood-burning brick oven. "Plain coffee or café au lait?"

"Doesn't matter." He glanced around the bakery absently as if trying to get his bearings.

"Well, of course it matters. Do you want cream or not?"

"Not."

"Then plain coffee it is. Take off your coat so that it'll dry out. As you can see, you have your choice of places to sit," she said, gesturing to the chairs around the four marble ice-cream tables up front. "Things are a little slow right now."

As if to mock her words, three customers came in the door. She waited on the first, and while two and three perused the goods, she quickly poured a cup of coffee for the man and set it on the table in front of him.

"There you go," she said. "Drink up. I'll be back in a shake with a refill."

After she'd rung up the final sale, she filled a tray with a basket of assorted rolls and pastries, a second mug, and an insulated carafe of coffee. When she started toward the man, she was struck again by the aura of desolation surrounding him. Strangely, she sensed that such feelings were ordinarily foreign to him. This guy was no wimp.

Even though he looked as if he'd lost his last friend, there was an air of authority and strength about him. And with his hair drying into a tousled gold crown, he was drop-dead, Hollywood handsome, barely saved from being pretty by a strongly chiseled jaw. Though he wasn't a muscle-bound brute, his shoulders filled his white dress shirt quite nicely. From his build, his tan, and the fairer sun streaks in his hair, she might have pegged him as a California surfer at first glance, but none of the ones she knew ever wore a suit or had enough depth to be morose about anything.

He didn't look up when she set down the tray. He remained seated in the white curlicued metal chair. With both hands wrapped around the mug, he stared into its contents.

"See anything in there?" she asked, sitting down across from him.

He glanced up, looking blank. "Pardon?"

She gave him her perkiest smile. "In your cup. You were studying it so carefully, I thought maybe you were reading it like Madame Zinora reads tea leaves." She held up the pot. "How about some more?"

He nodded and she poured.

She broke a roll, slathered it with butter and offered it to him. "Try it. We bake the best in the Quarter."

He took a bite. Then another. "Very good," he said politely, though he didn't seem to have his heart in it.

"Told you." She buttered the other half and gave it to him. "By the way, my name is Amy Jordan. What's yours?"

"Mud."

Startled for a moment, she recovered quickly and said, "Like Roger Mudd, the newscaster?"

"No, Mud with one *d*. At ten o'clock this morning I became a pariah, and my name is Mud."

"I don't understand."

"Neither do I." He stared down into his mug again. "None of it makes any sense. I ran those experiments a dozen times. The result was always the same. Now . . ."

Amy waited, but he didn't answer.

The bell over the entry tinkled, and the brief blare of a jazz trumpet slipped through the open door before it was closed again. Amy looked over her shoulder and nodded to the scruffy, skinny man who was none too clean and wore a tattered raincoat and a watch cap pulled low over his eyebrows.

She turned back to the man sitting across from her, struck anew by his sorrowful, arresting eyes and extraordinary good looks. Touching his arm lightly, she met his gaze and said, "If you'd like to talk about it, I'm told I'm a very good listener."

He raked his fingers through his hair, then glanced up at the ceiling. "God, I don't even know where to start."

"The beginning is always a good place. Or you can jump in anywhere, and we can work our way backward and forward from there." When he only looked at her and blew out a big breath, she smiled and said, "We can start with your real name. I know it isn't Mud."

"It's Larkin. Neil Larkin."

"I'm delighted to meet you, Neil Larkin."

She started to extend her hand to him, but he glanced sharply toward the door as the bell tinkled. Scowling, he yelled, "Hey, you!"

Before Amy could stop him, Neil jumped up and took off after the shabby fellow who'd been in the bakery. She hurried after them in time to see Neil tackle the fleeing man.

"What are you doing?" Amy shrieked.

Neil pushed himself to his feet. "He was stealing your bread. He hid it under his coat."

He glowered at the man on the ground who had drawn himself into a fetal position, his darting eyes wide with fear.

Amy laid her hand on Neil's arm. "This isn't *Les Misérables*." She helped the downed man to his feet and patted his back. "Sorry about the misunderstanding, Pullet. Are you okay?"

Pullet's head bobbed on his long, grimy neck, but he eyed Neil warily as he pulled three mashed baguettes from beneath his coat. "But the bread's all broke up."

Amy examined the loaves. "Oh, they're not too bad, but if you'll come back to Rachel's, I'll find you some others."

She steered the two men, who shot leery glances at each other, back to the bakery and replaced the three crushed baguettes with others and added a sourdough *pain* for good measure.

When the ragged little man had gone, Neil said, "Will you explain why you replaced a thief's damaged merchandise?"

She laughed. "Pullet's not a thief. He's a street person. When I found him rummaging in the alley garbage cans for old bread, I told him to come by at the end of the day, and we could cut out the middleman—or can in this case. By tomorrow morning all the bread on this table won't be good for much except for bread pudding or driving nails. I hate to see it go to waste."

Neil raked his fingers through his hair. "God, I feel like such a fool. This hasn't been my day."

"Good heavens, don't worry about the misunderstanding with Pullet. You were only trying to help. Have you had dinner? No, of course you haven't. I'll bet you missed lunch too. I'm starved, and I know that you must be. Coffee and a roll aren't substitutes for proper nourishment. Know what I'd like? A big bowl of seafood gumbo and a glass of wine. Doesn't that sound scrumptious? Why don't you go in the back and change into some dry clothes while I close up, and we'll go over to the Gumbo Shop and eat. Come on."

She picked up his suitcase and garment bag and started to the back of the store.

"Here, let me take those," he said, relieving her of the baggage. "Where do I go?"

She led him through the large kitchen and pushed open the door to a small room with a cot folded in one corner. "Here's a good place. This is where our baker Emile stays sometimes when he and his wife Felice have a fight. They haven't had any problems lately, so things may be a little dusty. Not from dirt," she interjected quickly, "but from flour. In a bakery, flour gets everywhere." She ran her finger over a small, scarred chest just inside the door. "Nope. Looks clean. Put on some jeans or something, and I'll go close up." She patted his arm and gave him her most reassuring smile. "Even though it might not seem like it at the time, things always get better. Especially if you have someone to talk to."

"You really believe that?"

"Yep. I'd rather believe that than the alternative."

Neil stood at the door and, shaking his head, watched her go, dark ponytail bobbing. He felt as if he'd been caught up in the maternal bosom of a whirlwind. Except that it wasn't the maternal appeal of Amy's bosom that struck him. She had a very nice bosom. In fact her whole body was very nice. About five and a half feet of very, very nice.

And she had one of the warmest smiles he'd encountered in a long, long time. So warm that he was almost sure that he could heat his hands by it. Her whole face became animated with dimples when she smiled—deep ones in her cheeks, two smaller ones at each corner of her mouth. Just being around her had made him feel a little lighter, made him forget for a moment—

Forget? How could he ever forget the towering humiliation he'd endured? No, it was more than mere humiliation. Embarrassment he could live with. His reputation, his credibility, his entire career had been shattered beyond redemption. He didn't know how to begin to pick up the pieces.

Since he had nothing better to do with the rest of his life, he put his suitcase on the chest and dug out the single pair of jeans he'd brought to New Orleans.

Amy spun the dial on the floor safe, switched the sign on the door to CLOSED, and fluffed her bangs. She turned to find Neil Larkin leaning against the doorjamb, fingers in his pockets, watching her with those arresting eyes. Her own widened appreciatively. If she thought he was handsome in a suit, he was practically illegal in low-riding jeans, white T-shirt, and a Windbreaker the exact baby-blue color of his eyes.

He looked down at himself. "Is this okay? I didn't bring much for casual wear."

"It's great! I mean, I like your jacket. Nice color."

"My sister gave it to me for Christmas."

"Oh, you have a sister?"

He looked amused. "I have three sisters. And two brothers."

"*Five* brothers and sisters! How on earth did you manage? I have only one sister, and she nearly drove me nuts when we were growing up. Oh, I love her dearly, and we get along okay now, but we're as different as daylight and darkness."

"We're all different, too, but somehow we rubbed along fairly well."

Outside, Amy gave Neil the poppy umbrella to hold while she locked the bakery door. He unfurled the petals and held it over them as they walked the short distance to the Gumbo Shop. To keep dry they had to stay close together, which led to her arm around his waist and his arm around hers. It seemed very natural, she thought as they avoided the puddles. And rather . . . intimate. Which was strange. She was a toucher. She'd always been a toucher. But touching Neil was somehow different. He sort of . . . vibrated. She hadn't a clue as to why. Maybe it was the drop in the barometric pressure. Or the music in the Quarter.

Her body automatically picked up the beat of the "Muskrat Ramble" coming from one of the clubs, and she jigged along to the tempo. "I just love Dixieland music, don't you?"

"I've never been very musical. Link says I'm tone-deaf."

"Who's Link?"

"My younger brother. He's a singer."

"Link. *Link Larkin?* He's your brother?"

"Yes. Have you heard of him?"

"Of course I've heard of Link Larkin. He's the hottest young country and western singer since Garth Brooks."

"Who's Garth Brooks?"

Aghast, Amy stopped and looked up at Neil. "You've never heard of Garth Brooks? What rock have you been hiding under?"

He shrugged. "No rock. I stay—stayed pretty wrapped up in my work."

"What kind of work?"

"I am—was a research biologist."

"Good Lord. With test tubes and slides and microscopes and the whole schmear?"

"The whole schmear. I . . . was in cancer research."

"How wonderful! I wasn't much good in biology. Especially lab. I felt so sorry for the poor little frog that I couldn't force myself to dissect him. If it hadn't been for my partner, I'd have probably flunked the course." She paused and looked up at him again. The haunted expression was back in his eyes. "You said *was*. Aren't you doing research anymore?"

"Not since ten o'clock this morning."

She urged him on toward the restaurant. "I want to hear the whole story. But first we're going to eat and have a couple of glasses of wine. Ummm. Smell that gumbo. Doesn't that make your mouth water like crazy?"

"It does smell good."

"It tastes just as good as it smells," she said as they went inside the Shop. "Scrumptious."

A few minutes later they were digging into big bowls of spicy gumbo filled with shrimp, crab, and sausage, accompanied by demi-baguettes of crusty bread. Amy noticed that Neil ate heartily.

"Good, huh?" she asked.

He looked faintly amused. "Scrumptious."

"What was it like growing up in a big family with three sisters and two brothers?"

"With six of us sharing a bathroom, what was it like? Loud. Hectic. Competitive."

"But loving, too, I imagine."

He nodded. "That too."

"Tell me about your family."

"Well, my parents retired last year and moved to California to be near my oldest sister, Peggy, and their only grandchildren. Peggy and her husband are entertainment attorneys. My brother Tom has a diving school in Florida."

"Diving? Like scuba diving?"

"No, like swimming pool diving. He trains Olympic hopefuls. He was a gold medalist."

"Gold medalist? As in Olympic gold medalist Tom Larkin?"

"He's the one."

"Well, what a small world." Amy grinned. "I watched him on TV. He's your brother?"

"Yes. And you might have seen my younger sister on TV as well. Sunny Larkin. She's a network correspondent in Washington."

"Of course I've seen her. She's dynamite. Wow, and with Link, your family is quite impressive." She counted on her fingers. "One sister is missing."

Neil chuckled. "Linda is definitely not missing. She and Link are twins, and she's his manager. She's the scrappiest one in the family and the power behind Link's success."

"Holy moley. I've never heard of so many high achievers in one family. Do you see one another often?"

"It's hard with everybody scattered all over the country, but we try to get together at least once a year, usually at Thanksgiving."

"That's only a month away. I'm sure you'll be glad to see them again."

A grim expression spread over his face. "I won't be going this year." He pushed his bowl away and drank deeply from his wineglass.

"Why ever not?"

"It would be awkward. I wouldn't want to embarrass them."

"Why in the world would you embarrass them? They're your family, and I'm sure they love you. Even Rachel, who thinks I'm hopeless, is always glad for me to visit."

He refilled their wineglasses. "But you've never done anything as stupid as I've done."

"Oh, no? Ask Rachel. She could recite a list of my dumb moves that would reach from here to Canal Street. Why, the only reason I'm here running the bakery while she's in Paris is because I got can—" She stopped abruptly when she saw the deep pain in his eyes. She reached across the table and took his hand. "Have you murdered someone? Have you committed some atrocious crime?"

He shook his head. "No. Nothing like that."

"Then tell me. Tell me about Neil Larkin."

He gulped another big swallow of wine, but he didn't let go of her hand. He kept his eyes on the table where he made slow circles with the bottom of his glass.

"Until this morning, I was Dr. Neil Larkin,

professor of biochemistry at one of the country's leading medical schools and, it was said, a sure contender for next year's Nobel prize for my breakthrough in cancer research." He glanced up, his eyes haunted by a pain so intense that it sucked her breath away and made her heart hurt.

"Go on," she said softly.

"After ten years' work in the lab, I'd found it. A compound that would revolutionize cancer treatment. To put it simply, I devised a substance that attacked and destroyed cancer cells very quickly with no damage to surrounding tissue and with no adverse effects. It was a miracle, Amy. A true miracle drug. God, I've never been so excited in my life. I sent copies of my studies to several colleagues around the country, and my findings were to be published next month in the *Journal of the American Medical Association.*

"Yesterday, I came to New Orleans with my research team and the head of my department to present my paper to America's most prestigious biomedical conference and receive an award."

"But, Neil, that's wonderful!"

His hand tightened around hers. "No, it's not wonderful." He tossed off the rest of his wine. "Not a single one of my colleagues could replicate my research."

TWO

Wide-eyed, Amy stared at Neil. "But why not? I'm sure you wouldn't cheat."

He gave a short, derisive laugh. "Thanks for that. At least someone believes in me. No, I didn't cheat. I wouldn't, even if I thought that by some miracle I could get away with it. As to why no one could replicate my research, I don't know." He shrugged. "Some bizarre fluke like the schizophrenic spider, I suppose."

"Schizophrenic spider?"

"It's a classic in research anomalies. Several years ago, a respected team was researching a possible physiological link in schizophrenia. They used a complex procedure, but simply put, they fed the blood of a schizophrenic patient to a spider, and—"

"And the spider spun a crazy, misshapen web," she said. "I remember that now."

"Their experiment was a major breakthrough that set the psychological community on its ear. Obviously, they surmised, something in the blood caused aberrant behavior. They had shown a clear physical basis for the mental condition, but—"

"No other laboratory was able to come up with the same results."

"Exactly," he said. "It was some sort of fluke. Even so, for years afterward their findings continued to be taught as fact in many Psychology 101 classes."

"Is that what happened in your research? Some kind of fluke?"

"There's no other explanation. But I repeated those experiments dozens of times. The probability of the same anomaly occurring with each trial strains the bounds of credibility. No, I don't think so."

"Could someone in your lab have tampered with the experiments?"

"For what purpose?"

Amy took another sip of her wine. "Revenge, envy, some personal desire to discredit you, any number of motivations."

Neil wrinkled his brow and turned the stem of his glass round and round with his thumb and middle finger. "I suppose that it's possible that someone has a grievance with me, but there was no opportunity for tampering. I conducted every single experiment personally or closely supervised the other members of my team. The laboratory was locked every night, and I had the only key. Because of the sensitivity of the work, not even the cleaning people were allowed into the lab without my being present. That's what looked so damning to my department head. I'm the only one who could have tampered with the materials."

Amy sat back in her chair and blew out an upward puff of air that fluttered her bangs. "Ho-ly mo-ley."

"Exactly." He poured another glass of wine and drained it.

"What could have happened?"

He shrugged. "I've racked my brain, and I can't come up with an answer. In my ten years there, nothing like this has occurred before."

"Well," she said huffily, "I think it's downright tacky of them to blame you for something you didn't do."

A smile slowly spread over his face, cutting a deep dimple in his left cheek. The smile expanded to brighten his eyes and crinkle their corners. If she'd thought he was handsome before, now she had to revise her evaluation to drop-dead, out-of-this-world gorgeous. His smile on full throttle could power the *Mississippi Queen*.

"I think it's kind of tacky myself." He reached across the table and gave her hand a little squeeze. "Thanks for the vote of confidence." He turned up the potency of his smile a notch, and she nearly slid off her chair. "Unfortunately the scientific community isn't so magnanimous. They think that, at the least, I'm a risky screwball and, at the most, a malicious fraud."

"Well, they must have rocks in their heads. You'll simply have to continue your work, figure out what happened, and show them all up."

"How? Nobody with the kind of facilities and funding it would take will hire me. As a scientist, I'm washed up. The news will race through the professional community like wildfire, and by tomorrow morning I doubt if I could get a job washing test tubes."

"It doesn't seem fair," Amy said, patting his hand.

"Maybe not, but those are the facts. And I have to do some hard thinking about what to do with the rest of my life."

He laid his other hand over hers and stroked it absently. At his touch she felt that tingly sensation again. It was like the hum of a tuning fork vibrating against her hand and running up her arm. Weird. But not unpleasant. Sort of exciting, she would say. What caused the sensation? Was it static electricity, or was it her reaction to this intriguing man?

Hoping that it was something as simple as static electricity, she eased her hand away and sipped her wine. He was much too handsome a man to even think about getting involved with. She'd been down that road before.

"That's what I've been doing," she said. "Trying to decide what to do with the rest of my life. My career is a bust too."

"What about the bakery?"

"Oh, that's just temporary. Rachel will be home next week. Working at the bakery is okay for the moment, but I have to decide what I'm going to do permanently. Going back to being a social worker is definitely out."

"Why?"

"Various reasons. After I trained forever to become one, I had a problem that lots of social workers run into. I'm a casualty of burnout. Plus my last supervisor said that I'm temperamentally unsuited to the field."

"And what does that mean?"

"It means that I can't distance myself emotionally from my work. I got too personally involved with my cases. I cared too much."

He frowned. "But caring seems commendable in a social service field."

"Not when you develop a spastic colon, migraine headaches, and stay broke from giving your salary away. Try as I might, I just couldn't fix everybody's problems. I'm a sucker for a sad story and a sponge for misery."

He gave her a distressed look. "And now I've dumped my sad story on you. Sorry."

"No problem. Compared to lots that I've heard, your problems aren't so bad. Nor are mine. We have our health, people who love us, good educations. We'll do okay." She patted his hand again. "Now let's forget all the downers for a while. My diagnosis for Dr. Larkin is that he needs to take a break and have some fun." She shoved her chair back, stood, and pulled him to his feet. "After all, this is New Orleans." Grinning broadly, she winked, snapped her fingers, and wiggled her shoulders. "Let the good times roll."

He chuckled and tossed money on the table for the check. "You're on. What do you suggest?"

"Well," she whispered conspiratorially, "I hear that there's a lady over on Bourbon Street who can do amazing things with strategically placed tassels."

❦ ⸺⸺⸺ ❦

When they left the club on Bourbon Street an hour later, Amy's eyes were huge and she had a stunned look on her face. Neil could barely contain his amusement.

"What did you think of her?" he asked.

"She certainly has an unusual talent. How do you suppose one develops such specialized muscle control?" She glanced down at her own breasts, frowned, and said, "Never in a million years could I—" She bit off her comment. "Well, whatever one thinks of the lady's profession, one has to admire her commitment to what must be a rigorous training schedule."

He burst into laughter. Amy Jordan was a delight, a charming concoction of ambiguity, both sophisticated and innocent. Even with his career around his ears, he couldn't remember when he'd had so much fun. It wasn't the strippers he'd found so entertaining; it was watching Amy's reaction to them, particularly the last one with the gyrating tassels. She'd tried to act blasé, but even in the dim light he hadn't missed her blushes. And every time that he thought that her eyes couldn't get any wider, they jacked open another notch. Watching Amy, being with Amy bolstered his spirits, made him feel like a kid again. And he hadn't felt like a kid in a long, long time.

"What next?" he asked.

"How about a cappuccino and some Dixieland?"

"Which way?"

She looked around. "We can try a place down on the next block. Okay?"

"I'm game." He unfurled the umbrella and held her to his side as they walked in the drizzling rain.

He liked the feel of her delicate warmth against him. He liked her smell—a subtle blend of yeast and sugar and spring flowers. He liked her smiles, her laughter, her spontaneity, the way she seemed to care about everybody and everything. In fact, he couldn't think of a single thing about Amy that he didn't like. He'd lost his job, but he'd found a friend.

More than a friend. They connected. A strange way to describe his feelings, but connected seemed to fit.

And she stirred sexual sparks inside him like no woman he could remember. Good, and not so good.

At the small club, they ordered cappuccinos and listened to wailing music that rattled the walls and shook his insides with fast-tripping blares and heavy bass beats. While it was true that he wasn't a musical aficionado, whatever it was about the rhythm that made everybody clap and sway and screw their faces into odd expressions affected him as well. The last knot in his stomach unkinked, and his mood shifted until his shoulders began to wiggle a little—maybe not exactly in tempo, but close.

Amy, who snapped her fingers and bounced on her chair as if she had motorized springs beneath her, noticed his movement. She grinned and bumped her shoulder against his. "Maybe there's hope for you yet. Any brother of Link Larkin's has to have a little rhythm in his bones and a hot streak down deep in his soul."

"Hot streak?" He laughed. Amy and the music seemed to inspire laughter and light-headedness. "I don't think Link has anything to worry about from me."

Between sets they talked. She told funny stories and laughed frequently. He found himself mesmerized by her expressive mouth, fascinated by a bit of whipped cream that clung to her upper lip. He was disappointed when her tongue flicked up and captured it, wishing that it were his tongue instead.

Dangerous thoughts, he told himself. Amy didn't strike him as the sort of woman who engaged in casual sex, and he wasn't in a position to let a relationship develop leisurely between them. He didn't even know where he'd be next week. Or tomorrow, for that matter.

He cleared his throat and glanced at his watch. "I think I'd better find myself a place to stay tonight. I checked out of my hotel."

She looked at her own watch. "It is getting late. You'll have a hard time finding a place tonight. You're welcome to stay in the little room off the kitchen. I know it's not grand, but the bed is comfortable."

"But, Amy, I'm practically a stranger. For all you know, I could pilfer the till and skip during the night."

She looked him up and down and smiled. "I'm a good judge of people. I trust you. You wouldn't steal anything, would you?"

"No, but you're too trusting for your own good."

Grinning, she said, "I've been told that frequently." She leaned close and whispered, "But if you're concerned, the money's in a safe that would take a dozen sticks of dynamite to open. You're welcome to all the leftover bread and pastries you can carry off. Emile will bake fresh in the morning. Oh, that might be a problem. Are you a sound sleeper?"

"I sleep like the proverbial log."

"Good, because Emile and Jimmy will be in early to bake. Just ignore them, and I'll leave a

note to let them know you're there." She stifled
a yawn. "How about we call it a night?"

He hesitated, hating for the night to end.
He'd probably be up and on his way early the
next morning. To somewhere. Probably back to
Houston to pack up his apartment and . . .
whatever.

They walked slowly back to the bakery.
Amy hated for the night to end. Behind that
handsome face, Neil Larkin was a very special
man, one she'd like to know better. But with
both of them in limbo and him off to heaven
knows where the next day, the timing couldn't
have been worse. She sighed deeply.

"Something wrong?" he asked.

"No. I was just thinking about . . . life.
Sometimes it can be a real bitch, can't it?"

"I'll second that."

Amy unlocked the door, and they went inside the shop. She wrote a note for Emile and
left it on his worktable so that he would notice
it first thing. When she turned around, Neil
was leaning against a counter, his hands in the
pockets of his Windbreaker, scrutinizing her.

"Well," she said, "that's taken care of."

He nodded.

"I suppose I'd better say good night and get along to bed."

"I suppose. Do you live far from here? It just occurred to me that it's late, and you shouldn't be out on the streets alone." He stepped closer to her.

She smiled. "No need to be concerned. I'm staying in Rachel's apartment." She pointed to a door. "Through there and upstairs over the shop."

He glanced to where she pointed. "Oh. Good."

They stared at each other, awkwardness filling the silence. "I—" they both said at the same time.

"You first," he said.

"I was just going to say that, if you leave early in the morning and I don't see you, it's been very nice meeting you, and I hope things turn out okay." She stuck out her hand.

Neil took her hand, but he didn't shake it. He clasped it between both of his and looked down at her, his eyes radiant as blue candle flames. "Amy, I can't begin to tell you how . . . how lucky I feel to have met you. At the risk of sounding corny, you've been like a guardian angel coming to my rescue. Thanks."

She felt herself go hot all over. Maybe it was the heat from his hands spreading over her, maybe it was the heat from the brick oven behind her, maybe it was the heat from his luminous eyes that seemed to sear into her brain, but she was very, very warm.

"I'm no angel, believe me, but if I was helpful, I'm glad." A huge lump suddenly formed in her throat, and she swallowed, trying to dislodge it. "Will you write to me and tell me how you're getting along? I don't know where I'll be after next week, but Rachel can forward a letter."

"Sure, I will."

Her throat tightened even more, but she smiled. "Good night then."

He smiled. "Good night."

He didn't let go of her hand, and she didn't, couldn't pull it away. They stood there for the longest time, smiling at each other, reluctant to part.

"May I have a good-bye kiss?" he asked softly.

An irrational impulse deep within her made her want to grab him in a stranglehold, plant a kiss on him that would melt a hole in a lab beaker, and hang on to him for dear life. Instead she answered with a breathy, "Yes," and lifted her face.

For a moment he didn't move. Then he brushed her cheek with the back of a finger, and his gaze scanned her features with such tender poignancy that tears rushed to her eyes. His lips lowered slowly to hers and touched them with the gentlest of kisses.

"Good-bye, Amy Jordan," he whispered an inch from her mouth.

"Good-bye, Neil Larkin," she whispered. "Have a good life." She moved away quickly to keep from making an idiot of herself by blubbering and clutching his shirt with a death grip.

She hurried to the stairway door and opened it, then turned to deliver a last smile. Shoulders slumped and hands in the pockets of his jeans, he stood where she'd left him. Their eyes met, and an overpowering sense of loss ripped through her as if she were saying good-bye forever to her dearest friend or a cherished lover. She sensed that they shared the same pain. Foolish, she told herself. Her vivid imagination running wild. Her confounded overly empathetic nature creating havoc again.

She forced herself to flash a perky smile and wiggled her fingers. " 'Night." She didn't wait for his response. Hurrying through the door, she closed it behind her and leaned back against it. Her heart was racing. She squeezed her eyes tightly shut and breathed deeply to keep from bursting into tears. What was the matter with her?

She heard Neil call her name very softly, and she yanked open the door. He hadn't moved. "Yes? Did you call me? Do you need something?"

"No. I just said . . . Amy."

"Oh. Well, good night again."

"Good night."

She tried to leave, but her feet wouldn't cooperate, and her eyes seemed locked into his by a dynamic force. Then she felt her feet begin to move, advancing her toward him as if she were a little pile of steel shavings being drawn to a magnet. She stopped in front of him, and he brushed her cheek again with the back of his finger.

"Oh, Amy, I wish . . ."

"What do you wish?"

"I wish I'd met you at a different time. I wish . . ."

"You wish?" Her voice was barely a whisper.

"I wish I could kiss you, really kiss you the way I'd like to."

"What's stopping you?"

"Circumstances. You're a confounding variable in my life right now."

"Sounds like a flimsy excuse to me." She lifted her face, licked her lips and parted them slightly.

"Don't do that."

"Do what?"

"Look so damned enticing."

She sighed. "Well, if the mountain won't come to Mohammed . . ." She grasped his nape, pulled his lips to hers, and kissed him for all she was worth.

He hesitated only a heartbeat before his arms went around her, and his mouth devoured hers like a starving man at a banquet. Bells clanged. Skyrockets exploded. The earth moved as if an entire Mardi Gras parade marched through the bakery. Her knees sagged, and she held on for dear life.

"Ho-ly mo-ley," she said when they came up for air. Every nerve ending in her body aquiver, she rested her head against his chest and tried to catch her breath.

"I was afraid of that," he said, his breathing as ragged as hers.

"Afraid of what?"

"Spontaneous combustion."

"You felt it too?"

"Oh, yes."

"Holy moley."

"Exactly." He unwound her arms from around him and led her to the stairs. "I think we'd better say good night for real this time."

"You're not going to kiss me again?"

"Amy, I—" He drew a deep breath. "No, I

don't think so. Good night." He practically shoved her toward the stairs and closed the door.

It took every ounce of fortitude she could muster to climb the stairs. It was going to be a long night. She doubted if she would sleep a wink.

Neil lay in bed blessing and cursing the timing of meeting Amy just when his life had gone to hell. What did he have to offer her? His reputation was ruined. He had no job, no prospects. Oh, he had enough assets to last several months, maybe even a year. But then what?

If he had a lick of sense, he'd get up and catch the first plane out of New Orleans. But the memory of Amy's lips against his, the sweet, soft feel of her body, the scent of her silky hair, the sound of her laughter bade otherwise. Something deep inside him whispered that Amy was special. Very, very special. And leaving now would be the worst thing he could do.

As a scientist, he'd never put much stock in things like fate or luck or other kinds of mumbo jumbo, but for once he was tempted to believe that events had conspired to throw him off his chosen track and bring him to this place in his life.

He could almost hear his grandmother's laughter at the turn his thoughts had taken. "One of these days, boy," she'd told him a dozen times before she'd died a few years before, "you're going to have to quit running and face up to who you are. Your sister wasn't the only one struck by lightning that day."

Thinking of his sister Sunny, he smiled. She was the hole in his scientific logic. He had no empirical basis for believing that she had a nose for news or could predict the weather with one hundred percent accuracy, but she could. She'd proven it over and over again. And she'd capitalized on her talents.

Disturbed by his train of thought, Neil pushed the memories in a back corner of his mind, but when he did, even more disturbing thoughts rushed in to take their place.

Amy.

The sweet, yeasty smells that clung to her skin surrounded him in the small room, filled his nostrils and stirred his emotions. He would never again be able to enter a bakery or eat a piece of French bread without thinking of her. Her smiling, dimpled face seemed imprinted in his brain; her taste lingered on his lips. He'd never met anyone who had such an immediate and profound effect on him. Something about her very essence burrowed under his skin and tugged at his heart.

Since an insurmountable wall had sprung up in his path, maybe it *was* time that he stopped running.

It wasn't as if he had anywhere better to go.

Maybe he would stick around a day or two and see what developed. He chuckled. *Maybe* hell. Who was he kidding? He was already concocting an excuse to stay.

THREE

The phone rang and jarred Amy from a deep sleep. She shot up straight in bed and glanced at the clock. Three-fifteen in the morning! Who could be calling at that hour? she wondered as she fumbled for the receiver. "Hello?"

"Miss Amy? This is Jimmy."

"Jimmy, where are you? What's wrong?"

"I'm in a phone booth down at the corner. The back door's locked, and Emile ain't there. I can't get in to heat up the oven. If I don't get the wood going pretty soon, we can't bake them pastries and loaves. And if we don't bake them, what am I gonna deliver?"

Panic flew over her. Dear Lord, where was Emile? Trying to remain calm, she splayed her hand across her chest and took a deep breath.

"I'll come down and let you in. I'm sure Emile will be along any minute."

"Yes'm. I'm coming."

Amy grabbed a pair of sweatpants and pulled them on under the oversize Dallas Cowboy jersey she slept in, hitching them up as her bare feet thumped on the wooden stairs.

By the time she unlocked the alley door, Jimmy was standing there waiting for her and looking worried. In his early twenties, Jimmy was a string bean of a kid with a big Adam's apple, an underslung jaw, and a bad overbite. While he was a little slow on the uptake, he was a conscientious worker and completely dependable.

"Emile ain't here yet?" he asked.

She shook her head.

With a finger, he tapped on the face of his cheap watch. "I was here at a quarter to three. Emile told me always to be here at a quarter to three, and I'm always here. He is, too, but he ain't here now. I waited and waited and knocked and knocked. I've got to put the wood in and get the fire going in the oven or he can't bake and I can't deliver. That's what he told me."

"You put the wood in, and let's give Emile another five to ten minutes to show up."

"Yes'm, but it ain't like Emile to be late. He

ain't never been late in all the years I been workin' here. Not never once."

"Maybe he had car trouble."

"What if he don't come? Can you bake the pastries and the loaves?"

"*Me?* Lord, no. All I know how to bake is chocolate chip cookies." Anxiety had raised her voice an octave. She tried to act calm for Jimmy's sake, but panic was gaining the upper hand. "Emile will be here. You'll see."

The words were barely out of her mouth when the phone rang. Her breath held, her fingers crossed, she answered. It was Felice, Emile's wife, and her words came out in a shrill rush.

"Slow down, Felice," Amy said. "I can't understand you." Her heart dropped to her stomach when she finally made out what the woman was saying. "How bad is it?" She listened to the tearful message, then said, "Thank God for that. Tell him not to worry. We have everything under control."

For the longest time, she sat there, the receiver to her ear, listening to the dial tone, too stunned to hang up. Dear God, what was she going to do? In a very few hours, bread had to be delivered to their customers and ready for the bakery shelves as well. She didn't have the foggiest notion as to how to begin.

"Emile coming?"

She shook her head. "He's been shot."

"Shot?" Jimmy's eyes widened. "Shot *dead*?"

"No. It's a shoulder wound, and he's going to be okay. He caught a couple of boys trying to steal his neighbor's car, shouted at them, and they shot him. Felice called from the hospital."

She dropped her head into her hands. What was she going to do? Customers would be furious, the business would suffer, and Rachel would kill her. Rachel. Should she call her sister in Paris? No, what good could she do from thousands of miles away?

"What we gonna do?" Jimmy asked.

"I haven't got a clue. Do you know how to make bread?"

He scratched his head. "Can't say that I do. Emile always mixes up the flour and stuff. I know how to put it in the oven and watch it. I do that sometimes. And I know how to turn up the proofer."

"The proofer? What's a proofer?"

"That thing back yonder. Emile made up this morning's pastry yesterday and put it in there. You turn it up, and they rise so you can bake them."

"Well, thank heavens for that. Turn up the proofer." Amy paced and tried to think. In her agitated state, her mind wouldn't function, but she managed to knock over a stack of pans that hit the floor with a loud racket. She scrambled to pick them up, whacked a huge stainless steel mixing bowl, and it flew off the counter, crashed on the floor, and rolled in a noisy clatter against the tall tray cart. "Is the fire going?"

"Yes'm. I put in the oak logs first thing. It's going good." He pointed to a spot on the temperature gauge outside the large brick oven. "When the arrow gets to here, we put in the pastry. When it gets to here"—he pointed to another spot—"we put in the bread."

"But we don't have any bread," she shrieked.

"Is there some sort of problem?" a voice asked.

Amy look up to see Neil, sleepy-eyed and rumple-haired, zipping his jeans as he came toward her. "Yes," she said, throwing herself into his arms. "I'm having a nervous breakdown."

He patted her back and made soothing noises. She tried to explain, but everything came out in a babble.

"Calm down," Neil said. "Take a few deep breaths, then tell me."

As best as she could while on the verge of hysteria, she related the situation. "And the only thing I know how to bake is chocolate chip cookies. What am I going to do? Rachel will kill me."

He chuckled. "I don't think so. We can handle it."

"We can?"

"Sure. A kitchen isn't too different from a laboratory. And I used to help my grandmother bake bread when I was a kid. The first thing we need is a recipe."

As Neil held her in his arms, a feeling of serenity settled over her. She grew relaxed, and her brain began to function. "Recipe. Rachel keeps her recipes in a book in the safe. I'll get it."

When she returned, Neil was talking with Jimmy and exploring the kitchen. He turned and smiled at her. When he did that something inside her melted. At that moment she couldn't have cared less about baking bread. She didn't care a whit if the whole of New Orleans had to eat cake instead.

He held out his arm to her, and she went to him like a falcon returning to its master. "Find it?" he asked.

She held out the three-ring binder to Neil. "Rachel guards this with her life. These are her special recipes."

He took the notebook and flipped through the pages, scanning them as he went. "This shouldn't be too difficult. Jimmy tells me that first we make baguettes, then *pain*. Draw some warm water while I crumble the yeast cakes."

"Shouldn't we read the recipes first?"

"I've read them."

"Holy moley. Are you a speed reader or something?"

He laughed. "Yes. But it's a relatively simple formula and not too different form the one my grandmother used. We just make more of everything."

When she returned with the water, Neil had crumbled yeast into several large mixing bowls. "Now we add sugar and salt." When he'd done that, he handed her a measuring cup. "Put this much warm water into each bowl and stir once. I'll assemble the other ingredients and figure out how the dough hooks work."

In a few minutes they had the first batches in the machines.

"Now what?" Amy asked as she watched the hooks knead the dough.

"Now we turn these out and let them rise while we mix the rest."

She grinned. "This isn't so hard."

"The secret is not to panic. First rule of the

kitchen." He laughed and brushed her nose. "Flour," he said.

She wiped her nose on her sleeve. "How long does the dough have to rise?"

"About an hour or until it doubles in size."

She checked the clock. "Thank God. An hour to rise, about an hour to assemble and bake, I think we're going to make it."

"That's for the first rising."

Her eyes widened. "What do you mean, *first* rising?"

"After it rises, we have to run it through this machine"—he pointed to a long conveyor contraption—"which flattens it and cuts it into strips. We shape the strips on the pans and let them rise again."

"For *another* hour?"

He nodded. "Using the proofer should cut down the time some."

"Ohmygod! We'll never make it!"

He grinned. "Remember the first rule of the kitchen."

"I will not panic. I will not panic. I will not panic. Ohmygod! We'll never get this bread out on time and Rachel will lose all her customers and she'll kill me!"

"Amy," he said softly, "trust me." He looked into her eyes with those heavenly baby-blues and touched her cheek.

Trust him? At that moment she would have followed him into hell without a canteen.

"Why don't you go check and see how Jimmy is doing with the pastries and the croissants?"

Jimmy was doing fine. He was just taking the last batch from the huge stone oven wheel with a wooden paddle and looking enormously pleased with himself.

"Don't these look fine, Miss Amy? Mr. Neil told me just what to do, and I did it."

"Very nice, Jimmy. Very nice."

"Pretty soon the oven will be just right for them loaves you're making. The heat's gotta be just right for them, and I gotta keep water in this little spout. Makes them nice and crusty, you know."

Amy chewed her lip and checked the time. "I know."

When she walked back to the area where Neil was, he was busy turning a big blob of dough onto the conveyor. "What are you doing?"

"I'm about to cut this dough into loaves."

"But—but—" she sputtered. "But I thought it had to rise for an hour to double in size. It hasn't been five minutes."

He shrugged. "Must have been a lively batch of yeast. It's ready. Look."

She peered into the other bowls, and sure enough, the dough was fat and puffy. Leaning close to one bowl, she squinted at it, then poked it with her finger. It fell away from her finger and deflated slightly. According to Rachel's directions, it was ready.

Peculiar. Very peculiar. She shrugged. What did she know?

While she'd been studying the bowl, Neil had already prepared two pans of loaves and was working on a third. She watched his agile fingers handle the dough as delicately as if it were a baby. He had beautiful hands with long supple fingers. It took only the slightest leap in her musings to imagine those hands against her skin, touching, patting, kneading—

She shook her head before her imagination went completely out of bounds and glanced up to find his eyes on her. She'd never thought of blue eyes being able to smolder. Black eyes smoldered. But his smoldered with a blue-hot intensity that made her tingle and shiver. She'd caught him looking at her that way a couple of times, and it made her nervous. Extremely nervous. She'd never met anyone who upset her equilibrium the way Neil did.

Fidgeting, she broke eye contact and said, "What can I do to help?"

"Turn on the regular oven over there. We need to make muffins and eclairs while the bread is baking."

"Can't we bake them in the brick oven?"

"No, they require a different treatment. Thank God we don't have to make cakes today."

"*Cakes?* We have to make *cakes*?"

He laughed. "Not for a couple of days yet. Jimmy said that Emile makes cakes twice a week, and he baked a supply yesterday. But we might have to make napoleons. We'll check the inventory when we've finished with the more immediate concerns."

Amy slumped against the counter where he was deftly shaping baguettes. "I'm already tired just thinking about it."

Neil leaned over and kissed her nose. "You're tired because you haven't had any sleep."

She sighed. "That too. But neither have you. Thank heavens Zelda will be here at six-thirty to handle the shop, and we can get a little sack time when we finish. I'm pooped, and I know that you must be too. We're going to have to go to bed earlier tonight—" She stopped when the reality of the situation hit her. Panic began to scramble upward again. "Ohmygod!"

He frowned. "What's wrong?"

"I said 'we' and assumed . . . but you won't be here tomorrow. What am I going to do? I can't handle all this by myself. And I can't ask you—"

He touched his finger to her lips and smiled. "I'll be here tomorrow . . . and for as long as you need me."

A warm, fuzzy feeling cocooned her, and she relaxed. "Thank you, Neil."

"My pleasure." He slipped the last of the pans into the tall tray cart slots. "While these are rising, why don't we make the muffins?"

Following Rachel's recipes, she made bran and he made blueberry, and by the time they were in the oven, the baguettes and *pain* had risen.

Amy checked the time, then looked back at the loaves. "Boy this yeast is something. It hardly took any time for them to rise."

He shrugged. "Ask Jimmy to put them in the oven, and I'll start on the eclairs."

By the time Zelda arrived to open the shop at six-thirty, Jimmy was out making the first deliveries, and the eclair shells had cooled and were ready to be filled and frosted.

Zelda, a wiry little woman with salt-and-pepper hair permed into tight curls, energy to spare, and a no-nonsense manner, took one look at the two ersatz bakers and said, "Where's Emile?"

Amy introduced Neil and explained the situation.

"Amy, you look like something that the cat dragged in. Why don't you two get some rest, and I'll call my sister-in-law to fill in for your shift till Emile's back or till Rachel comes home."

"Oh, Zelda, would you? I'd be eternally grateful."

"Sure. Esther Ann works here sometimes when Rachel needs an extra hand. She knows the ropes." She lowered her voice and leaned closer. "I'll count the eclairs before she comes on. She's got a weakness for them, you know."

Amy chuckled and whispered, "So do I." She gave Zelda's arm a squeeze and thanked her again. "As soon as we finish the eclairs and clean up, we'll leave things to you." Zelda went to open the front door, and Amy turned back to Neil. She was surprised to find that all the shells were filled and he was starting to frost them with chocolate. "Boy, you're fast."

He winked. "Comes from working my way through college in a pizza parlor."

"Did you really?" She began helping with the frosting.

"I really did. I worked at a pizza parlor, drove a florist delivery truck, and sold shoes, among other things."

"I figured, as smart as you are, you had a scholarship."

"I did, but I worked for clothes and spending money. With six of us kids, my parents couldn't help much. We all worked."

When the last of the eclairs was done, Amy dragged her finger through the frosting bowl and licked the blob from her finger. "Ah, heavenly." She scooped another dollop and started toward her mouth.

Neil grasped her wrist and brought it to his mouth instead. His gaze locked with hers, and he slowly drew her finger into his mouth, licking it clean. "Very tasty." Slowly, like a cat, he licked it again. "Very tasty."

Her knees buckled. She'd never known that her finger was an erogenous zone, but she felt heat stir low in her belly and spread upward to warm her throat and flush her cheeks. Alarmed by her reaction, she jerked her finger away and averted her gaze. "Uh, we still have to make the pastries for tomorrow and clean up."

She began moving things around on the

counter, making no improvement on the mess whatsoever.

"Amy." Neil stilled her busy hands and turned her shoulders toward him. "You don't have to be afraid of me."

"Afraid? I'm not afraid of you. You just make me nervous when you look at me like that."

"And how do I look at you?"

"Like you'd like to eat me up."

He smiled. "I would, but I won't."

She didn't know whether to be relieved or disappointed. "And when you touch me . . . my stomach does flip-flops. I'm not so sure that it's a good idea for you to stay. Maybe I—"

He released her immediately and held up his hands, palms out. "Then I won't touch you unless you want me to. But you need help, and I'd like to reciprocate your kindness to me. Okay?"

Taking a deep breath, she blew it out in a bang-ruffling puff. "Okay. But I'll pay you for your work here. I don't know exactly how much Emile makes, but—"

He suppressed her words with a finger to her lips and one of those heart-stopping smiles. "Friends don't take money for helping friends. You're very tired. Why don't you go up to bed?"

"But the pastries. And the place is a mess."

She waved her hand over the dirty bowls and utensils.

"Part of Jimmy's job is to clean up, and we can make the pastries later today."

Overcome with fatigue, she agreed. She trudged upstairs, fell into bed, and slept as if she were drugged.

Neil couldn't sleep. Amy filled his mind. When in panic she'd thrown herself in his arms, he'd felt ten feet tall. And he'd been excruciatingly aware that she'd been braless beneath the oversize football jersey she wore. Merely thinking about it made his body stir. He hadn't had such a case of raging hormones since he'd been sixteen.

If anyone had asked him why she affected him so, he couldn't have explained why he found her so sexy, but he did. Even her bare toes turned him on. She made him feel as if he'd awakened from a twenty-year sleep, excited and eager to experience the world.

He was sorry that the baker had been injured, but he was grateful that he had an excuse to hang around. Amy needed him. The skills he'd learned in his Creole grandmother's kitchen had returned easily, and the years of efficient laboratory experience made the baking a simple task.

Along with the trick with the bread dough.

He chuckled. He never dreamed that his little quirk would come in handy one day.

FOUR

For Neil, the four days he'd spent at the bakery had passed both quickly and slowly. Quickly, in that he and Amy had been so busy baking and stocking merchandise, ordering supplies, keeping books, and settling into a comfortable routine that they'd hardly had time to breathe. Slowly, in that every day Amy burrowed deeper into his skin until he was aching for her.

He hadn't kissed her again after that first night. He wanted to. God, how he wanted to. But kissing her when he thought there would be no tomorrow, and kissing her now that they were under the same roof were two different things. He had a hunch that if he kissed her the way he wanted to, he'd probably frighten her out of her wits. He didn't want to stop with merely a few kisses. His fantasies were filled with images of her under him, hot and moaning his name.

Even now, watching her ice napoleons, he could hardly keep his hands off her. Each time they were close, each time they accidentally brushed hands or hips, a jolt shot through him that kept his jaws sore from gritting his teeth. He didn't know if she felt the same way, but it seemed to him as if every atom in the room vibrated with a new intensity when she was near.

His gaze swept over her, and with no trouble at all, he could envision those lovely long legs beneath her swirling skirt, bare and wound around him. He almost groaned aloud at the thought and tried to harness his mind, but his eyes remained on her skirt, spellbound, fantasizing, wishing . . .

With a swipe of her forearm, Amy mopped a sheen of perspiration from beneath her bangs. She could feel Neil's eyes on her. In the few days since he'd come, her internal thermostat had gone haywire. Nowadays she never knew if the room was too warm or if she was suffering from a chemical imbalance. If she'd been older, she would have attributed her condition to hot flashes, but thirty-one was too young for menopause. She'd finally figured out that with him around, she stayed perpetually warm. Sometimes even when he wasn't around, she felt downright steamy. Those were the times when he filled her thoughts.

She wondered why he hadn't kissed her again, but she decided that it was for the best. If he ever made a move, she'd probably frighten the poor man to death by dragging him to bed. Ordinarily, she was only mildly concerned with sex, especially with someone she barely knew. But lately all she could think about was sex.

With Neil.

Tamping down her recalcitrant libido, she focused on icing the napoleons.

She felt a sudden draft around her legs and glanced down. Her gauzy calf-length skirt had ridden up over her knees. Puzzled, she batted at it and shook the fabric until it dropped back into place.

After a few moments she felt it creep up again, inching slowly over her knees. And higher.

Slapping at it again, she glanced over her shoulder and asked Neil, "Is there a fan on?"

He didn't answer for a few seconds. The mixing bowl and whisk he held were stilled, and his gaze was locked on her legs. His jaws were clinched, and there was a strange, faraway look in his eyes.

"Neil?"

He glanced up. "Yes?"

"Is there a fan on somewhere?"

"No, I don't think so."

"Oh." Her skirt settled around her calves, and she went back to her task.

After a few moments, she felt her skirt begin to creep up again as if being lifted by marionette strings. She batted at it, but it crept higher and higher until a goodly expanse of thigh was visible along one leg.

Slapping at the fabric irritably, she said, "What is going on here?" She whirled around to face Neil, who had a preoccupied expression on his face and was staring at her bare legs. "Neil! What is going on?"

He glanced up. "Pardon?"

"Something strange is happening. My skirt keeps riding up."

He looked taken aback. Clearing his throat, he said, "Static electricity perhaps." He turned his back to her and began beating the whisk like crazy.

She looked down at her skirt. The fabric lay in gauzy swirls around her calves. She plucked at it, and it fell back into place. Static electricity? She frowned. If so, it was the strangest acting static electricity she'd ever encountered.

Checking her skirt several times to see if it was behaving—and it was—she finished the napoleons, transferred them onto a paper-lined tray, and carried them from the kitchen to the shop.

Esther Ann, who was as Humpty-Dumpty plump as her sister-in-law Zelda was thin, was waiting on a customer. Her graying blond hair pulled into a fat bun, Esther Ann had a cherubic face that was perpetually flushed and a tiny little voice that seemed at odds with her body bulk. "Oh, look at those napoleons. Don't they look scrumptious? Sir," she said to the customer, "they're fresh from the oven. Wouldn't you like to have a half dozen?" She smiled sweetly.

The man started, then studied the tray. "Why, yes I think I would. My mother is quite fond of those."

Esther Ann beamed and boxed them up.

When the man left, Amy laughed. "Esther Ann, you're a treasure. And a born salesperson. Thanks for helping us out."

"Oh, I was glad to do it. With all my children gone a long way off, I don't have much to do with myself except to sit around and crochet and watch my soap operas. I've made so many doilies and tablecloths and bedspreads that I can do it in my sleep. I like getting out. Speaking of getting out, are you and Neil still going to see Emile at the hospital?"

"Yes, we're leaving in a few minutes. Today is the first breather we've had. After we see Emile, I thought we might play hookey for a few hours. Are you sure you don't mind closing if we're late getting back?"

"Not one bit. I know exactly what to do. Now you and your young man run along and have a nice time. You two make such a handsome couple. Makes me wish I was a girl again." She sighed.

"Oh," Amy said, "but we're not a couple. I mean—"

Esther Ann smiled knowingly and wagged her finger. "Now don't try to fool me. I've seen the way you two look at each other. Why the room grows positively warm when those sparks start shooting between you."

Amy's eyes widened. "You've felt it too?"

The grandmotherly woman chuckled. "In a manner of speaking."

They made a brief visit to the hospital to see Emile, who was so grumpy that Felice was wringing her hands. He informed them that he was being released the following day and would return to work no more than a week later.

After leaving the hospital, Amy drove her little red car along Canal Street, then cut over toward the Central Business District, pointing out sites to Neil as they headed to the Riverwalk.

"My grandmother grew up not too far from her," Neil said.

"Here? In New Orleans?"

He nodded. "In the Garden District."

"Wow. That's a beautiful part of town. The big old houses there are lovely."

"So she said. I never saw the place. Nor did she after she was eighteen."

"What happened?"

"She fell in love with my grandfather. Her family objected to her marrying him, said he was dirt poor and beneath her station. But Gran was an independent sort. She married him anyway and moved to north Louisiana. Her parents disowned her, and she never saw them again."

"How sad. She must have loved your grandfather very much."

"She did. And they had a happy life. They had one son, my father, and three daughters. Gran and I were always very close, a special bond, I suppose." He smiled. "She's the one I used to help make bread."

"Is she still living?" Amy asked.

"No. She died when I was a freshman in college. Cancer."

As he did occasionally, he seemed to withdraw and turned to stare out the window. Amy sensed that he didn't want to talk anymore and kept quiet until they arrived at the parking lot. Although he hadn't mentioned it again, she knew that the disaster with his research still troubled him deeply. At odd moments over the past few days, she'd caught him gazing into space, a frown wrinkling his brow. She could almost hear the cogwheels in his brain turning, desperately searching for an answer to the dilemma posed by his research catastrophe.

She wanted to help, but she didn't know how. She bit her tongue to keep from prying further. Being on the river would do him good. Her too. She'd booked a sunset excursion on one of the riverboats. It was something she'd always wanted to do when she visited New Orleans but had never gotten around to doing.

They parked and wandered around the grounds of the Riverwalk Marketplace until time for departure. He became a little more talkative as they enjoyed the balmy day outdoors after spending so many hours cooped up in the bakery. By the time they went up the gangplank, he was laughing again.

As soon as the triple-decked stern-wheeler pulled away from the dock, Amy excused herself to powder her nose. When she returned, she found Neil leaning against the rail on his forearms, his hands clasped out in front of him, staring at the muddy Mississippi. A breeze ruffled his hair and tugged at his shirt. He looked a million miles away again.

She joined him at the railing, imitating his posture by leaning against the top rung on her forearms. "Neil, what's wrong?"

"You mean other than the fact that my reputation is ruined, and I've been booted out of the position I've worked twenty years to attain?"

"Right. Stupid question."

He turned to her and gently tucked a flyaway strand of hair behind her ear. "Sorry. I don't mean to be such a grouch. I guess that seeing Emile today and realizing that he and Rachel will be back to take over the bakery next week, plus thinking about Gran brought it all tumbling back around my ears."

"Neil, I can't believe that things won't work out. Somehow you'll be able to prove that you're not a cheat."

He cupped her chin, smiled indulgently, and kissed her nose. "My eternal optimist. No, Amy, I'll never have that chance. I've explained that no reputable institution will hire me now."

"But you don't know that for sure."

"I know."

"Then you'll just have to do it independently."

"And where will I get the funding?"

She opened her mouth, then closed it. After a moment's hesitation she declared, "I don't know, but I'll think of something. You can't just . . . just give up!"

"And what are you going to do the rest of your life now that you've given up social work?"

She cocked an eyebrow. "That was a low blow."

"You're right. Sorry."

"Oh, don't look so hangdog about it. You're absolutely right. I have to make some decisions. And I've been thinking about it. Helping people is what's important to me. There are lots of areas involving social services or charities where I could be of value. Maybe something administrative. Or I could be a lobbyist or a fund-raiser. I'm very persuasive, you know."

"I know. Just look at what you roped me into doing. How many bakers have a Ph.D.?"

Feeling chagrined by his comments, she tensed and searched his face to see if he was serious. "Oh, Neil, I'm sorry. Do you feel I've coerced you into something beneath you?"

He smiled and hugged her against his side.

"Relax, I was only teasing. I'm exactly where I choose to be right now. Let's forget all this heavy stuff and enjoy the sunset."

They turned back to the railing and watched the setting sun paint the water, changing the muddy Mississippi into a wide ribbon of shimmering gold. She held her face to the damp breeze laden with the earthy scent of the river and the more pungent odors of industrial civilization.

Twilight descended with a soft flurry of settling waterfowl and a gradual blinking on of lights along the shore. With evening came a slight chill that sent a rush of goose bumps over her skin, and she shivered.

Neil hugged her shoulders. "Ready to go inside for dinner?"

"Yes. I'm famished."

A few minutes later they sat at a candlelit table, their plates heaped with Creole and Cajun food from the lavish buffet.

"Mmmm," Amy said. "Doesn't this look fabulous?"

"Do you think you can eat all that?"

She gave him a saucy grin and started peeling crawfish. "You may have to roll me down the gangplank when we dock, but I'm going to give it my best shot. Eat up. I don't want to be the only one making a pig of myself."

He laughed. "You're good for me, Amy Jordan. You're the best thing that's come into my life for a long, long time."

She felt that peculiar warmth she'd been experiencing lately steal over her. His words, the expression on his handsome face spawned a bubbly giddiness inside that made her want to laugh and whirl around and hug herself. Or him.

She took a sip of her wine to calm the bees buzzing in her stomach. "Why did you decide to go into cancer research?"

"Because of Gran. She was too young to have died such a terrible, lingering death. Too young, too loving, too vibrant. Her death was senseless. It made me angry."

"What did you plan to do before . . . she died?"

"I was going to major in business, become an entrepreneur, make piles of money, and live the good life. When I was eighteen, my greatest ambition was to have a shiny new black BMW convertible."

"And you traded your dream to go into research. That's commendable."

He chuckled and looked a little sheepish. "Actually, I bought myself a BMW convertible a couple of years ago."

"Well good for you." She patted his hand and beamed.

"Maybe not. Now I'm wondering how I'm going to keep up the payments."

During the meal, Neil devoted more attention to Amy than he did to his food. She had such a marvelous zest for everything she did, including eating. Her presence perked up his spirit and made him feel carefree.

He watched as she sucked the insides from a boiled crawfish and imagined that it was his tongue that she tugged on. She licked her lips, and he ached to lean across the table and taste that lush mouth, rosy and shining from buttery juices. The more he watched, the more erotic her actions seemed, the more aroused he felt himself growing.

"Aren't you going to eat your oysters?" she asked, liberally dousing hers with hot sauce.

He shook his head.

She grinned and stretched forward toward him, her breasts brushing the tabletop. "You know what they say, don't you?" she whispered. "Raw oysters are supposed to be an aphrodisiac."

He laughed. He didn't need any help from oysters. The soft shape of her breasts, even hidden by the zippered sweater she wore, were aphrodisiac enough.

He became fascinated with that sweater, that zipper. The sweater was red, the zipper gold with a little gold ring attached to the tab. It was unzipped to modestly show a couple of inches of smooth silky skin below the hollow of her throat.

His finger itched to grasp that little gold ring and slip it down, down until her breasts were revealed, lush and bare to his mouth. How he ached to slide it down . . . down . . .

Amy felt a tug at her sweater. She glanced down and was horrified to see the lace of her bra showing almost to her nipples. Slapping her hand to her chest, she looked quickly to Neil to see if he'd noticed. He had. His eyes were glued to her bosom.

"Oops," she said lightly, fumbling to restore her modesty. "Must have caught on something."

He didn't say a word. Nor did she comment further. Self-consciously, she kept her eyes on her plate and continued eating.

After a moment or two, she felt another tug and looked. The zipper was easing down again. She stopped breathing, deliberately concaved her chest to release any pressure on the sweater. Still the zipper crept slowly down the track. She glanced at Neil, who was staring, seemingly mesmerized, at the rebellious zipper. She felt it sliding down, down, farther and farther.

She peeked at the zipper, then at Neil, then back to the zipper. The gold ring stood out at a forty-five degree angle, and the tab continued to move slowly downward, the spreading teeth revealing more and more of her bra. She didn't move. An improbable, impossible notion struck her. She dismissed it. It cropped up again.

"Neil," she whispered.

He didn't respond.

"Neil!"

He glanced up.

The zipper paused.

Her heart almost stopped, and she felt blood drain from her face. "Oh . . . my . . . God."

Neil looked alarmed. "Amy, what's the matter? Are you ill?"

Unable to speak, she waved him away, yanked her zipper to the top of its track, and grabbed her wineglass. She downed the contents in one long gulp.

She plunked the glass on the table and drew a deep breath. "You did it, didn't you?"

"Did what? What are you talking about?"

"My zipper! I'm talking about my—" Realizing that she'd raised her voice to a shriek and people were staring, she leaned forward and whispered loudly, "I'm talking about my zipper. You were pulling it down!"

"Amy, I haven't touched your zipper."

"I don't mean with your hands. I mean with— Ohmygod! My skirt. It wasn't static electricity. It was you!"

FIVE

A puzzled expression on his face, Neil said, "I don't know what you're talking about."

Amy looked heavenward. "Give me a break, Neil Larkin. I'm talking about zippers that unzip without being touched. I'm talking about skirts that creep up for no reason. I'm talking psychokinesis."

"Psychokinesis?"

"Psychokinesis. The ability to move objects with the power of your mind."

He shifted in his chair as if he were extremely uncomfortable. "I understand the term. But surely you're not suggesting that I—"

She narrowed her eyes. "Let's say that my working hypothesis is that you're psychokinetic."

"Amy, there's absolutely no scientific evidence to support such a notion."

"But of course there is. I've read about some Russian women who have done it in the laboratory."

"The stringency of their experimental conditions have been called into question. Other variables may have been responsible for their being able to move matches and small cylinders."

"Aha!" She gestured triumphantly with a finger high in the air. "You've read about it. Why?" she asked, narrowing her eyes and leaning closer. She pecked her finger on the table. "I'll bet you dollars to doughnuts that it's because you wanted to find out about others like you!"

"Shhh, Amy," he said, glancing around, "people are staring."

"Oh. Sorry." She scanned nearby diners self-consciously, then sat back and took a sip of water. She leaned close again and whispered, "You *are*. Admit it."

"I'm admitting nothing. That's foolishness. Ask any reputable scientist."

"Fie on reputable scientists." Snatching an empty oyster shell from her plate, she plunked it on the table between them. "Move that. I double-dog dare you."

He picked it up and put it back on her plate.

She rolled her eyes. "Don't be difficult." She replaced the shell. "Use your mind."

"Amy, I can't—"

"Okay, okay, maybe an oyster shell is too heavy. Let's start with something smaller." She pinched off a tiny piece of her roll and put it in place of the shell. "Try that little bit of bread and— Oh . . . my . . . God." An eerie sensation rippled over her as another realization struck her. "It was you."

"What?"

"Our baker's yeast isn't unusual. It's *you* who makes the dough rise so quickly."

His gaze shifted from hers.

"What? No denials?"

Silence.

"Come on. Give."

Obviously uncomfortable, Neil said, "Can't we discuss this later? Finish your dinner."

"I've lost my appetite."

"Because you think I may be some kind of freak?"

"Certainly not! What kind of person do you think I am? I think the whole idea is exciting. Wow." She slumped back in her chair and grinned. "Wow. Imagine being able to do something like that. Fantastic."

He grimaced. "It doesn't rank up there with being able to find a cure for cancer."

"Then you admit it. You're psychokinetic!"

"Shhh, Amy. If you'll wait until we're alone, I'll explain."

She jumped up. "Then let's go."

"We have to wait until the boat docks."

"Oh." She sat back down again and began to fidget.

Amy made sure that they were the first ones off the gangplank. She was dying of curiosity.

As soon as they were in her car, she turned to Neil and said, "I'm going to burst if I have to wait another minute."

He grinned. "Oh, I doubt that."

"Ne-il!"

"Really, Amy, it's no big deal."

"Being psychokinetic is no big deal? Who are you kidding?"

"I'm *not* psychokinetic. I merely have some quirk that enables me to make bread rise faster than normal. My ability isn't of great consequence. I rarely think about it, and I haven't done it in years."

"How did it start?"

"When I was a kid. It's a long story."

"I'm not moving this car until I hear the whole thing, so you might as well spill it."

He made an exasperated sound and laid his head back against the seat. "When I was about seven or eight and my sister Sunny was about four, we were caught outside in a thunderstorm. We took shelter under a big oak tree and lightning struck it, split it in half, and lifted us off the ground. The soles of our sneakers melted, and I still have burn scars on my chest from where the metal snaps on my shirt fused shut. I was only dazed, but Sunny was unconscious for several days. Everybody was very worried about her."

"But she was okay. Of course she was okay. I see her on television all the time."

"Yes, she recovered, but God, I felt so guilty. Sunny was so little, and she always followed me around like a puppy. I should have had better sense than to stand under a tree. It was a huge relief when she came around. There didn't seem to be any lingering physical effects, but we both ended up changed."

"How?"

"Sunny developed an odd ability to predict the weather, and I—"

"Became psychokinetic."

"No, I could make bread dough rise. That's all. My grandmother was the first person who noticed. As I told you I used to help her in the kitchen."

Restless with excitement, Amy wiggled into a more comfortable position in the cramped space of the little car. "What happened the first time?"

"I was alone in the kitchen with Gran a couple of months after the lightning incident. We were making her special cinnamon rolls, my favorite. Like most kids, I was impatient to have one, but my grandmother reminded me that we had to let the dough rise first. I remember sitting on a stool, my elbows on the counter, staring at that bowl with my mouth already watering. For me, an hour was an eternity. I wished and wished that the dough would hurry. In my mind I imagined it rising faster and faster.

"It did. Gran didn't catch on at first, but when dough kept rising quickly when I was around, she realized what was happening." He chuckled. "She used to call me her 'dough boy.' My brother Tom, who's only a year older than I am, used to call me worse. He teased me unmercifully."

"Does anyone else in your family have special abilities?" she asked.

"Not the kind you're talking about. Sunny and I are the only odd ducks. That's why we assumed that, in some way we don't understand, the lightning must have caused it."

"You're not odd ducks. You have special gifts."

"You sound like Gran. Sunny capitalized on her talent, if you want to call it that. I tried to forget about mine. I didn't like being called a weirdo."

"You've never explored your abilities further? Does anybody know about what you can do?"

"No and no. Except my family. It's not the sort of topic one brings up in casual conversation. May we go home now? I'm tired."

All the way back to the bakery Amy's mind raced a mile a minute. Whether he would admit it or not, Neil *was* psychokinetic. And he could do more than make dough rise. She was convinced that his mind had lifted her skirt and slid down her zipper.

Once inside, she took his hand and practically dragged him into the kitchen. She dug through her purse until she found a ballpoint pen. She uncapped it, plunked the smooth cylinder on the counter, then stood back, her arms folded across her chest. "Make it move," she challenged.

"Why?"

"You're the scientist. Don't you have the basic curiosity all scientists are supposed to have?"

"Of course. But I don't really think I can. In any case, of what earthly value is being able to move a pen with mind power? Do you know the story of the holy man who spent his entire life learning to walk on water so that he could cross the river?"

She frowned. "The one where his master told him it was dumb to waste a lifetime learning the trick when he could have ridden the ferry for a nickel?"

Neil smiled. "A slight corruption of the story, but that's the general idea."

"I get the message," Amy said impatiently. "But we're doing some basic research here that will take only a couple of minutes. We can worry about applications later. Won't you at least try it?"

He hesitated.

"Come on," she said. "Humor me."

Their eyes met, hers pleading, his wary. Then his softened, and he smiled. He brushed her cheek. "Only for you, Amy Jordan. Only for you."

While she watched, heart pounding, he turned his attention to the pen on the counter. For a moment nothing happened, then his jaw tightened, and she could see his features strain slightly.

Seconds ticked by that seemed like hours.

Was the pen moving or was it her imagination?

No, it moved.

She held her breath.

A quarter turn.

Then another.

And another.

It rolled slowly across the counter, fell over the edge, and bounced on the floor at her feet.

Her eyes wide, she stared at the pen lying not two inches from her toes. Her breath left with a *whoosh*. She lifted her gaze to his. "Ho-ly mo-ley," she whispered. "Ho-ly mo-ley."

"My God!" Neil exclaimed, looking stunned.

"You did it!" Squealing and bouncing up and down, she threw her arms around him. "You did it! You did it!" She planted kisses all over his face. "I can't believe it. It's wonderful! You're wonderful!" Laughing, she rained more quick kisses over his face.

For the longest time Neil couldn't move. Neither arms, nor legs, nor brain seemed to function. Dazed, he stood rooted to the spot.

Then gradually he became aware of the familiar yeasty smells of Amy's arms around him, her breasts pressing against him, her lovely, liquid eyes shining up at him, her lush lips smiling.

His total attention became focused on those lips. Lips he'd ached for since the time he'd kissed her that first night. Lips that haunted his dreams and plagued his waking hours. Lowering his head, he captured their sweet softness. His arms went around her, and he dragged her close while his tongue thrust between her teeth to find hers. He held on to her as if she were an anchor to reality and kissed her with all the pent-up hunger that was in him. And his hunger was formidable. He felt ravenous, insatiable.

When she moaned against his mouth, an answering feral sound shuddered in his throat, and he held her tighter, kissed her more fervently with a powerful passion that strained at the leash of civility like a half-tamed tiger. Instinctual urges welled up inside him, swelled and grew until he wanted to growl and roar.

He kneaded her buttocks and pulled them closer, sucked at her tongue, and nipped with his teeth wanting more, more.

When she moaned again and pushed at his shoulders, he startled, then stopped, reluctantly but immediately. Realizing that he was crushing her, he relaxed his hold. "Oh, God, I'm sorry. Did I hurt you?"

"Just a little." Her breath was ragged. His was more so.

He released her and turned away, ran his fingers through his hair and sucked in great gulps of air. "Please forgive me. I don't know what got into me. I never meant to hurt you."

Her hand on his shoulder was gentle, and it stroked small, soothing circles. "I know you didn't. Don't worry about it. It was the . . . uh, exhilaration of the moment I imagine."

For a long while neither of them spoke. Then he drew a deep breath and said, "It's getting late, and we have to get up at two-thirty. We'd better get some sleep."

"Yes, we'd better get some sleep."

Amy couldn't have slept a wink if her life depended on it. She was wired like a time bomb. Not only was her body throbbing and wrestling with a hormonal frenzy caused by Neil's passionate onslaught, but her mind raced like the lead car at Indy. What an evening it had been. Her thoughts skipped from Neil's kiss to the pen rolling off the table, then back again. Five more minutes, and they would have been stripped and rolling on the floor. Holy moley, the man was lethal.

Such power in him. And not just sexual power. His mind was a "Believe It or Not" phenomenon.

Neil hadn't been nearly as delighted about the pen as she'd been. In fact, he'd acted shocked. Was it possible that he really hadn't realized before that he was psychokinetic? Well, he was. For sure.

Lord, how exciting! If she'd been the one able to move that pen, she'd still be jumping up and down. But Neil was so darned pragmatic. The scientist in him, she supposed. So what if he couldn't see a practical application? She'd bet she could come up with one if she put her mind to it. She was great with creative ideas.

Challenged, the wheels in her brain started spinning.

She glanced at the clock and groaned. She had to get some sleep. She'd be dead tomorrow if she didn't. But her thoughts went round and round like a roulette wheel.

Forcing herself to use the familiar standby of relaxation techniques, she tensed and released muscle groups starting with her toes. When her entire body was relaxed, she focused on letting her mind wind down slowly, slowly

. . . like a wheel gradually coming to a halt until a ball dropped—

She gasped and jackknifed straight up in bed.

She had it!

SIX

By midmorning Jimmy had long since made all his deliveries and gone home; the bakery was stocked and filled with the tantalizing aromas of fresh-baked breads and the tangy sweetness of fruit-filled pastries; new supplies had been ordered, and Zelda handled the front of the shop with her usual efficiency. Neil slid the last tray of croissants for the following day into the proofer while Amy made a final notation in the account book.

Amy tossed down her pencil, stood, and stretched. "I can't believe we're done for the day. We're actually done."

Neil took off his baker's apron and hung it up. "I think we've got this thing down to a fine art." He walked closer to her and scanned her face. He reached as if to touch her cheek but drew back his hand and crammed it in his pocket. He'd neither touched her nor mentioned anything about what had happened the night before. She hadn't brought it up either.

"You look tired," he said. "Why don't you go up and take a nap? I know I could use one."

"I'm tempted, but there are some other things I want to do today. While you're napping, I'm going to do a little shopping in the Quarter, grab a quick lunch, and go to the library or a couple of bookstores."

"Maybe I'll go with you, if you don't mind my tagging along. I could use something to read."

She hesitated only a second, then smiled. "No, I don't mind." She didn't really. In fact she loved his company. But she wondered how he'd feel about the objective of her shopping expedition. Or the place she intended to shop. "Give me a shake to get presentable, and we'll go. Hollis will be on the square today. A few minutes with him will fix us right up."

"Who's Hollis?"

She smiled mysteriously. "A surprise."

Outside the bakery, which faced the small, fenced expanse of green park that served as the hub of the Vieux Carré, Neil asked, "Now are you going to tell me who Hollis is?"

"Nope. I told you, it's a surprise. Isn't it a glorious day?"

Warm, with a few fleecy clouds far above the cathedral spires, the day was lovely. A slight breeze rustled the palm fronds and banana leaves and stirred the flowers flanking General Jackson who sat atop his bronze horse in the center of the square. The air quivered with a legacy of gaiety, with a cacophony of vibrant sounds and enticing smells, some sugary and light, others spicy and robust. Only the muggy humidity, a perpetual New Orleans curse, kept it from being absolutely perfect.

Several artists had hung their paintings and sketches along the cast-iron fence surrounding the square, various vendors offered their wares from pushcarts, hustling passersby and trying to ignore the loud, impassioned orations from a couple of competing speakers on their soapboxes. A juggler with a clown face entertained a small group, and a wrinkled man with old, old eyes and sagging pants played blues on his saxophone for donations into his open case.

Amy bit back a giggle at Neil's expression when he spotted Hollis's sidewalk concession on one corner of the square. The folding sign offered: SOOTHING NECK AND SHOULDER MASSAGES—$10, WITH HEALING CRYSTALS—$12.50.

"What kind of screwball is he?" Neil asked, scowling.

"Just your regular run-of-the-mill sort typical to the area. Come on. Don't be a spoilsport. It's my treat." She tugged at his hand. "Hi, Hollis," Amy called when they came near. "Got time for a couple of customers?"

"Always for you, love." The short, muscled man with the dark Vandyke beard and crew cut took her hand, bowed, and kissed her fingertips. "When is Rachel coming home?"

"Two more days." Amy glanced at Neil, who looked decidedly uncomfortable. "You want to go first or shall I?"

"Uh, you go first."

She grinned and plopped down in a deck chair under the awning. "Let's shoot the works, Hollis." She handed him twenty-five dollars. "I'm a mess, and I need some energy."

Hollis studied her for a moment, then taped a stone to her forehead and gave her one to hold in each hand. He slipped a CD in the portable player and fixed headphones to her ears. "Close your eyes, love, and flow with the music."

His hands began to gently massage her neck and shoulders. And she was gone.

The next thing she knew, the music no longer played and Hollis was shaking her gently. "How does that feel, love?"

She stretched and smiled. "Fantastic. Like eight hours' sleep." She glanced around for Neil. He stood to one side looking as if he were waiting his turn at the guillotine. "You're up." She stood and offered him her chair.

"I think I'll pass."

"Oh, no, you don't," she said, laughing and pushing him into the seat. "Trust me. It's wonderful." To Hollis she said, "He's a mess too."

Hollis cocked one dark brow, giving him a close perusal. "A mess, yes, I can see that. But he's such a handsome devil."

Amy bit back a giggle at the licentious gleam in Hollis's eye. If it had been anybody else, she might have felt jealous, but she was confident of Neil's sexual orientation. She had to agree, though, that Neil *was* a handsome devil, especially in the jeans and light blue shirt he wore—part of a purchase of additional casual clothes he'd bought a couple of days before.

"Sit down," Hollis said. "I think I'll use the lapis with you."

As they walked along Chartres headed toward downtown, Amy said, "Tell me the truth, didn't Hollis make you feel wonderful?"

He mumbled something.

"I didn't understand you."

"It was okay."

She laughed and bumped her hip against his. "You lie . . . and your nose is growing. You feel great, admit it."

He shrugged, but a smile played around his mouth.

She bumped his hip again. "Admit it, you hardheaded pragmatist."

He laughed. "Okay, I admit it. I'm just glad that none of my colleagues could see—" His words halted; his smile died.

"Stop that." She poked him. "Forget about all those old fuddy-duddies and their sanctimonious pronouncements. You're going to show them. You're going to rub their noses in it. Today is the first day of your exciting new life."

His eyebrows went up. "Do you know something that I don't?"

She smiled mysteriously. "I may. Wait and see."

"Exactly where are we going?"

She glanced up at the street signs. "It shouldn't be too far. Here, we turn right on St.

Peter and . . . there it is." She pointed down the street.

"There what is?"

"The Purple Unicorn. It's a sort of bookstore. Hollis recommended it."

When they stopped in front of the small shop with a purple door, Neil looked at her strangely. Crystals of all shapes, sizes, and shades hung in the window along with displays of tarot card decks and bundles of dried herbs. A small sign on an easel announced: PSYCHIC READINGS, INQUIRE WITHIN.

"It's not like any bookstore I've ever seen," he said, eyeing the place with a frown.

"Then prepare yourself for a new experience." She opened the door, which set off a tinkling of glassy bells, hooked Neil's elbow with hers, and practically dragged him inside.

No one was in the shop except an older woman with a profusion of Lucille Ball red hair who was attending to a display of miniature unicorns with a feather duster. She wore a long, gauzy muumuu, blue with silver stars and tiny mirrors sewn onto it. She turned as they entered and smiled, her mouth a starburst where magenta lipstick had bled into the wrinkles around her lips.

"Come in, come in," she said. "I am Madame La Belle, the proprietor. Have you come for a reading?"

Amy could feel Neil tense beside her. "Uh, no. We're looking for a book."

"Ahhh. I have the finest metaphysical selection in New Orleans. In the back, through here." Her green eyes twinkling as if with hidden amusement, she held back strings of beads hanging in a doorway. "They are arranged by topic."

Neil looked as if Amy were dragging him into the bowels of Hades, but he allowed her to tow him along.

Once in the stacks, he said, "This place is damned spooky. What are you looking for?"

"Shhh. A book."

"The books on psychokinesis are right in front of you," Madame La Belle's voice rang out from beyond the curtain. "Second shelf from the bottom."

"Dammit, you told her!" he said.

Wide-eyed, Amy whispered, "No, I didn't. I've never seen or talked to the woman in my life. I didn't even know this place was here. All I did was ask Hollis where I could find some books on parapsychology. That's it, I swear."

"Well, it's damned weird if you ask me."

She pursed her lips to keep from laughing and selected three books and two pamphlets that appeared to be helpful. She handed them to Neil. "That ought to do it."

When they returned to the front part of the shop, Madame La Belle awaited them at the cash register. She took the books from Neil and glanced at the titles as she rang them up. "Very good selections." She placed the books in a purple shopping bag and while Amy was writing a check, the woman said to Neil, "May I hold your hands for just a moment?"

Amy glanced at Neil who looked as if she'd asked him to grab a rattlesnake. "Why?" he asked.

Madame laughed merrily. "Just call it an old lady's whim." She held out her hands to him, palm up.

He hesitated, then shrugged and placed his hands in hers.

"Ahhh," she said after a moment. "I thought so. Such *power*." She withdrew her hands and smiled. "I have something for you." She went to a glass case, removed an object, then came back and offered it to Neil. "For you. A gift." A smooth wooden disk about the size of a half dollar, it had a zigzag pattern carved on one side. "A small thing, but one with extraordinary vibrations. It was made from a tree split by lightning. Carry it in your pocket" —she glanced at Amy and winked—"for luck."

She laughed gaily as if at some internal joke and handed him the bag. "Come again."

Outside, he turned to Amy and held out the disk. "If you didn't say anything to her, how do you explain this?"

Amy widened her eyes and shrugged innocently. Truthfully, the entire episode had left her a little shaky, but she would have denied it to Neil under torture. "I have no idea. Swear to God."

Eyeing her skeptically, he crammed the disk in his pocket. "If you ask me, it's damned bizarre. That woman made my skin crawl. Let's get out of here."

She was only too glad to agree. "I'm hungry. How about we stop somewhere for a *muffuletta?*"

"Fine with me. Why did you buy those books?"

"I just want to know more about the subject. I should think that you would too."

"As I said, I can't see much of a practical application, and I'm darned sure not about to put on a turban and go on the stage. God forbid that I should end up as spooky as Madame La Belle. Let's talk about something else."

Amy sensed that the time wasn't right to tell him about her idea. He seemed pretty touchy about his ability. She would wait until she had done a little more research before she sprang it on him.

After lunch, they walked downtown and stopped in a bookstore that was part of a national chain. "Is this normal enough for you?" she asked.

"It's more my speed."

They split up to make their selections. Amy was careful to get to the register with hers before Neil could see what she was buying.

When they left the bookstore, they caught a cable car and rode it awhile, just for fun, then rode another back to town. They strolled back to the Quarter at a leisurely pace, stopping to browse in shops that caught their fancy and to buy an ice-cream cone to eat as they walked.

"I love New Orleans," she said between licks of her strawberry cone, "but if I lived here all the time, I would weigh six hundred pounds. Food here is so bodaciously delicious that all I do is eat."

Neil laughed. "And here I was thinking about asking if you wanted to go someplace special for dinner tonight."

"Don't let what I said stop you."

"Very well. Would you like to go someplace

special for dinner tonight? We could make it later."

"Sounds wonderful. But not too late. Two-thirty in the morning comes awfully early. Lord, I'll be glad when Rachel comes home. I'm a night person. Are you?"

"No, ordinarily I'm an early riser." He smiled. "But closer to six than two-thirty."

At the bakery Esther Ann had things well in hand, and she shooed them away. They parted with Neil intending to read the novel he'd bought and Amy chomping at the bit to peruse her purchases upstairs in private. "Are you sure you don't want to read one of the books we got at Madame's?"

"Positive. I prefer Tom Clancy."

First Amy scanned the material on psycho-kinesis, marking any passages she wanted to study more in depth. Actually, she didn't dis-cover much that she didn't already know. There were all sorts of theories about why certain in-dividuals possessed such abilities, some more crackpot than others. Basically, it boiled down to the fact that nobody really understood why certain people could move things with their minds. She did learn that kinetic facilities seemed to work better if positive believers were present—that was her—and they usually improved with practice. Interesting.

Several sources reported a downside to psychokinesis. It exacted a physical toll, in some more than others. In short, in its own way, moving objects with the mind was as strenuous as weight lifting and taxed the physical body and its systems with elevations in heart rate, blood pressure, and so forth. Important to remember.

Amy put the first batch of books aside and was about to reach for the ones she'd bought downtown when there was a knock on her bedroom door.

"Amy, I'm going to take a shower now," Neil called out. "Want to leave in about an hour?"

"Okay," she called back.

Since there was only a half bath off the little room downstairs, Neil had been coming upstairs to use Rachel's shower. It didn't present a problem since there was another bathroom off her bedroom.

Day after tomorrow, things would change. Rachel would be back from Paris to reclaim her bakery and her bathroom. While Amy knew that her sister would be content for her to stay on, at least for a while, Neil would feel superfluous.

He would leave.

And go where?

What if she never saw him again?

An ache shot through her heart, and her throat tightened. She couldn't let him simply ride off into the sunset. Alone. He'd get all depressed again.

She pulled a book from the second sack and thumbed the pages. She smiled as the idea, which had germinated the night before, took root and began to grow. Checking her watch, she allotted herself twenty more minutes before she had to get dressed.

She turned to the first page of *The Basics of Casino Gambling* and began to read.

Day after tomorrow, Neil thought. Where had the time gone? It seemed only yesterday that Amy had dragged him into the bakery and plied him with coffee and pastry. Only yesterday in one sense, but a lifetime ago in another.

He rubbed his hair to dry it, wiped the steam from the mirror, and knotted the towel around his waist. Looking into the mirror, he felt his chin and decided to shave again.

He squirted a handful of foam, then paused before he lathered it on and looked carefully at his reflection. It was the same face he'd shaved for years, yet something was different. Something he couldn't quite put his finger on. He leaned closer, trying to figure out what it was.

Something about the eyes. The set of his mouth.

His eyes seemed brighter; his mouth, more relaxed.

At first he attributed the changes to meeting Amy, but he felt that it was more than that. What, he didn't know. Hell, maybe that session with Hollis did him more good than he wanted to admit.

But no, come to think of it, he'd seen the same face in the mirror yesterday that he was seeing now. It couldn't be that he was more rested. He hadn't had a decent night's sleep since he'd been here. But something was different.

He shrugged and slapped the lather on. He had more pressing problems to consider. Such as how he was going to find a way to land in the same place that Amy went—if she ever figured out where she was going. Amy was like a willow in the wind. Every time he'd tried to pin her down about her plans, he'd failed. Tonight, he'd decided, he was going to be more persistent.

Neil had arranged for a horse-drawn carriage to pick them up at the edge of the square and take them the short distance to the restaurant he'd selected. She'd never looked more beautiful, he thought as he helped her into the seat. Her eyes shone and her hair, done up in a style that left little wispy curls around her lovely face, matched the elegance of her simple black dress and high-heeled sandals. For a moment, the notion occurred to him that she needed diamonds at her ears and on her fingers, and he wished that he could whip out a jewel case to provide them for her.

"How *delightful*," she said, holding her face to the gentle evening breeze from the river. "And how sweet of you to have thought of it." She smiled and touched his arm. "Neil Larkin, I think you're a romantic at heart."

He laughed. "I've never been accused of that before. But I thought you might enjoy it."

"You were right." She kissed his cheek and settled against him for the few blocks' ride to the Court of Two Sisters.

They dined in the lush courtyard lit by ornamental lampposts and flickering candlelight. Soft music and the ripple of cascading water from a tiered fountain provided the background for their sumptuous meal and fine wine. If their relationship had been a little farther along, Neil thought, this would be the perfect spot for a proposal.

Two weeks ago, such a notion would have never entered his mind. But two weeks ago, he hadn't met Amy. His entire world had been his work.

His work.

The thought of his laboratory being directed by someone else, the disgrace of the conference didn't bring the smothering pain that it had a few days before.

Strange.

He refocused his attention on Amy—which wasn't difficult. The flickering candle flame shot bits of gold through her dark eyes, eyes that drew him into their depths. He covered her hand with his as it lay on the pristine tablecloth, stroked it and marveled at its softness.

"Any decisions about where you'll go, what you'll do after Rachel returns?" he asked.

She glanced down, breaking eye contact. "Not exactly. It depends."

"Depends on what?"

"Oh, I don't know. A lot of things. What about you? Where are you going? What are you going to do?"

"Oh, I don't know. It depends."

"On what?"

He smiled. "On you."

She gave a little gasp, and her big, beautiful eyes widened. "On *me*?"

He nodded. "You must have figured out by now that I have more than a passing interest in you."

"You do?" Her smile could have lit the courtyard with its sunshine.

"I do. So you see, my plans depend on yours. Any hint of what I might expect?"

"Well, I thought I might take a vacation for a week or two."

"Sounds good. Any particular destination?"

"Ohhhh . . . maybe Mexico. Maybe . . . Las Vegas." She took a sip of wine. "Las Vegas sounds sort of appealing. Have you ever been there?"

He shook his head. "Have you?"

"Once about three years ago I went with some friends. I lost my shirt at the slots. Well, not exactly my shirt, but I blew my budget. Even so, we had lots of fun there." She looked at him sharply. "Ever done any gambling?"

"Not to speak of. In college I played penny-ante poker occasionally. I buy a lottery ticket once in a while. That's about it."

"So you're not philosophically opposed to gambling or anything?"

She looked so serious that he had to chuckle. "No. But the stock market is a better investment for your money. Want some dessert?"

"Heavens no. I don't know where I'd put it."

They lingered over a final cup of coffee, then decided to walk the few blocks home and stop for a nightcap on their way.

Arms around each other's waists, they strolled among the tourists, catching snatches of music and conversation spilling from the various clubs along their route. Although it was getting late for them, the Quarter seemed to be just getting started. Neil didn't know if it was the energy of the area, the woman beside him, or both, but he felt more alive than he could remember. Excitement seemed to crackle around them and spark an inner surge of anticipation.

He threw back his head, breathed deeply of the heavy evening air, and hugged Amy closer. "God, I feel good. Like I could run a marathon."

She laughed. "Don't try it now. I could never keep up in these heels. Want to stop by Pat O'Brien's for a Hurricane? It's just up ahead."

"A Hurricane? It sounds deadly."

"You mean you've *never* had a Hurricane?"

"Not that I recall."

"Come on then," she said. "You can't leave New Orleans without drinking one. It's a tradition."

The place was packed, but they crowded in and found a place at the bar where two women played rousing music on a pair of ornate pianos and incited the mob to raucous hilarity.

Halfway through their first Hurricane Punch, Amy felt decidedly mellow. Halfway through their second, both she and Neil joined in a bawdy song led by the piano players, singing loudly and laughing uproariously.

Since her face was going numb, she didn't finish her second but he continued to suck on his straw until he slurped the bottom and ordered a third.

She giggled when he started going down on the last potent concoction. "Don't do it. You'll turn into a zombie. Trust me. Hurricanes are notorious for sneaking up on you and laying you flat. We'd better go home."

He gave her a sappy grin. "Your wish is my command." He rose and made a flourishing gesture which sent his glass flying. He staggered slightly and blinked. "Oops."

"Oops." A little snort of laughter burst from

her as she tried to stand. "Me too. Oops." She giggled and grabbed his shoulder.

Laughing and hanging on to each other, they managed to make it outside. Neil stood on the curb and looked up and down the block. "I think your carriage turned into a pimpkin."

She snickered. "*Pump*-kin."

" 'S what I said. I don't see a carriage any . . . where."

"We'll walk." She took two wobbly steps, and her knees buckled. "Oops," she said, clutching his arm.

"Oops," he said, laughing hilariously.

They made it to the end of the block before her ankles started giving way. "Gotta get out of these heels," she said, perching on a fire hydrant and bending down to slip them off.

Neil knelt at her feet to help her. His hand stroked her nylon-covered ankle, then her calf. "But you'll ruin the beautiful stockings on your beautiful legs. Have I told you that you have beautiful legs?"

She shook her head, then stopped when his image went fuzzy.

"They're beau-ti-ful. Very sexy. I look at them every chance I get." He grinned and wiggled his eyebrows in a parody of lasciviousness. "And that's not all I do."

She leaned her forehead against his. "What else do you do?"

His grin widened. "I'm not telling. But I do it. A lot. Come on, it's not that far. I'll carry you." He stood and reached for her.

"Neil, you can't carry me. I'm too heavy."

He lifted her into his arms. "Naw, you're light as a feather."

"*Neil*, put me down. People are staring."

"Who cares? Let them stare."

After a block, he was breathing hard. Staggering a few more steps, he sat down on the base of a fountain with her in his arms.

Snickering, she tucked her head under his chin. "Told you I was too heavy. Let me walk."

"No. You're *not* too heavy, and I'm in great shape. I work out three times a week. It must have been the Hurricanes. Just let me rest a minute, and I'll be fine." He kissed the top of her head and snuggled her close. "I like this better anyhow."

His hand slid along her ankle, her calf, her knee. When his fingers slipped halfway up her thigh, she slapped her hand down, trapping his. "*Neil*," she squealed. "We're in public."

He grinned. "Then let's go home so we can be in private." He rose with her still in his arms.

"Put me down and let me walk."

"Nope." He stood her on the fountain rim

and turned his back. "Climb on. I'll be your steed. Come on. Put your legs around my waist and hang on."

Giggling as he swayed slightly, she climbed on his back. "Giddyap!"

"Hi-yo, Silver! Away!" He galloped toward Jackson Square, dodging tourists and locals, with the pair of them hooting and laughing louder than anybody.

When they reached the bakery, she giggled and yelled, "Whoa, horsey!"

He whinnied and backed up to a bench so that she could dismount. Once she was off, they collapsed against each other in a fit of hilarity.

"Do you care that we've made spectacles of ourselves?" she asked between giggles.

He touched his forehead to hers. "Not a damned bit. It's been a blast." Another sputter of laughter spewed from him, and he drew her closer against him. "God, I love the way you feel."

He started to kiss her, but she laughed and ducked. After fishing for the key in her small shoulder bag and fumbling with the lock, she opened the door and grabbed his hand. "Come upstairs with me. I want to try something."

A sappy grin spread across his face. "I'm game. Anything. Anyplace. I'm yours to command."

Getting upstairs took longer than usual because Neil suddenly seemed to have more arms than an octopus, all bent on touching her intimately. He nipped her ear and nuzzled her neck until she almost forgot her destination.

And when he kissed her at the top of the landing, her brain turned as gushy as a raw oyster.

"Oh, God, Amy," he moaned and started to kiss her again.

"Wait, wait." Her fingertips halted his lips. "We need to do something first."

He frowned, a foggy expression on his face, and swayed. "What?"

She giggled. "You'll see. I have a simply splendid idea."

He grinned. "Me too." He shucked his coat, let it drop to the floor.

SEVEN

Amy knelt on the floor of Rachel's bedroom, backside in the air, peering into the bottom shelf of a bookcase. Neil got on his hands and knees beside her.

"What are we looking for?" he asked, his face close to hers.

"Ah, here it is," she said. Feeling triumphant that she'd located it, she smugly held up the box for Neil to see.

"Monopoly?" He eyed the game as if it were a fish five days out of water. "You want to play Monopoly? *Now?*"

She tried to stifle a giggle at his expression, but failed miserably. "Not exactly. I want to try an experiment."

"Me too. But if it's games you want, how

about strip poker?" His eyes brightened, and he traced the scooped neckline of her dress.

"*Ne-il!* You're drunk as a skunk. Pay attention to me."

"I'm not all that drunk. I'm paying attention to you. I pay attention to you all the time. To your legs, your body, your eyes, your lips. Especially your lips." With her holding the box between them, he leaned close and marked the outline of her mouth with his tongue. "They're so soft. Give me a kiss, love."

"Not until we try my experiment."

"After that will you kiss me?"

"We'll see."

He sighed and sat back. "Let's do it."

She opened the box and laid out the board on the floor. She picked up the die, sat back on her heels and frowned. "There really ought to be a pair of these, but one will have to do."

He stretched out on his stomach with his chin in his hands. "Are you going to be the banker?"

"We're not going to play Monopoly."

"Good, I'd rather kiss you. Come here." He started crawling across the board, lips puckered.

"Neil!" She pushed him back. "I swear you have a one-track mind. I told you that we're going to do an experiment. Now this is the way it goes: I'm going to throw the die, and I want you to make it land on six. Psychokinetically."

"Why?"

She rolled her eyes heavenward. "You're not going to make this easy, are you?"

"All I asked was why."

She sighed and thought for a minute. "I've got it. Here's the deal." She picked up a stack of play money and counted out five hundred dollars in front of him. "We're going to play a game. I'm going to roll the die. If it lands on six, I'll give you another hundred dollars. If it lands on anything else, I'll take one of yours away. Okay?"

"Let's play this another time. Right now I'd rather kiss you." He moved toward her with a devilish gleam in his eye.

"Wait! Tell you what, if you collect a thousand dollars, I'll give you a kiss guaranteed to curl your toes."

"Promise?"

"Promise."

He chucked his shoes, yanked off his tie, and grinned. "Roll 'em."

She shook the die carefully and tossed it on the board. It landed on Reading Railroad. A four.

"Damn!" he said as she collected a hundred dollars from his stack.

She shook it again and threw.

A five.

"I'm not doing too well," he said. "Think it was that last Hurricane? Things are kind of fuzzy."

"Just concentrate." She threw the die again.

A six.

He grinned.

A one.

He spat out a succinct oath.

Eyes wide, Amy splayed her hand across her chest. "Why, Doctah Lahkin," she drawled in her best imitation of a Southern belle, "Ah didn't know you knew such words. You must not want to kiss li'l ole me very badly."

"The hell I don't. Roll 'em."

A six.

A six.

A three. Another oath.

A six.

A six.

A six.

He grinned.

Another four. The same oath.

Then four sixes in a row.

"A thousand dollars," he said, waving the cash. He handed her the sheaf of play bills. "Time for the payoff." He pulled her from the floor and into his arms. "Curl my toes, sweet-heart."

She did her darnedest. But it was her toes that curled. He kissed her with a potency that left her boneless. Hundred-dollar bills floated to the floor around them.

She could only stand helpless, unable to move as he trailed kisses all over her face. He nipped her earlobe and drew its shape with his tongue. All the while his hands stroked her, gently, but with a touch like none she'd ever felt.

With a single fluid movement, he unzipped the back of her dress, and his fingers played over her bare skin. When she would have pro-tested, his lips captured hers and the wicked things he did with his tongue sent her soaring.

The next thing she knew, her dress was in a puddle on the floor, and they were lying across Rachel's bed with Neil's lips on the swell of her breasts.

She pushed at him. "Neil, stop. I—"

He kissed her briefly. "Shhh. I won't do anything you don't want. Just let me hold you for a minute. Just for a minute more."

A raucous sound jerked Amy awake. She lay curled against Neil, who was still dressed in his shirt and slacks. She was in her black teddy. Her heart hammered as she tried to remember—

The phone rang, and she fumbled for it. "Hello."

"Amy, this is Jimmy. I'm down the street in a phone booth again. Door's locked, and I can't get in."

"Ohmygod! I'll be right there." She slammed down the phone and shook Neil. "Wake up!"

He mumbled and drew her back into the cradle of his arms.

Flailing from his hold, she shook him and yelled, "Get up. We have bread to bake."

He opened bleary eyes and sat up. Grabbing his temples, he groaned and flopped back down. "Dear God, what's wrong with my head?"

"Rum," she said, laughing. "You've got a lulu of a hangover. But we've overslept, and I need to go downstairs to let Jimmy in."

"God, I feel like elephants are stomping grapes inside my head. Did I do anything foolish last night?"

"Don't you remember?"

"Only vaguely." He looked at her, then around the room. "Did I—? Did we—?"

She only smiled. "I have to go downstairs. Soak you head in some cold water and take a couple of aspirin. It may help." She laughed. "Then again, it may not."

After a hectic few hours getting everything out on time, at last Amy and Neil could work leisurely on the pastries and croissants to be stored in the proofer until the following morning.

"Is your head any better?" Amy asked, hesitating to mention that he looked like something the cat dragged in.

"Only marginally. Do you feel as rotten as I do?"

"Nope. But I didn't have as much to drink as you did."

"Sorry if I made a fool of myself. I seem to remember galloping through the Quarter with you on my back. Did I really do that?"

"Yes." She smiled. "But it was fun."

He chuckled. "It was, wasn't it?" When the last tray was filled, he said casually, "I remember playing some strange form of Monopoly, then kissing you. Everything after that is blank. Did we . . . ?"

She smiled mysteriously. "I'll never tell."

"We didn't."

"How can you be so sure?"

"You still had on your panty hose this morning."

She winked. "I wore a garter belt."

He groaned.

She laughed. "I'll put these in the proofer. You take some more aspirin and go back to bed. You look ghastly."

"I feel ghastly. I think I will go back to bed. What are your plans?"

"Oh, I might go out and knock around some in the Quarter. It's a beautiful day." She kissed his cheek. "You rest."

Neil went to his little cubbyhole, and Amy went upstairs to shower and change.

Before Amy left the bakery, she checked with Zelda, who had everything under control. She was about to go out the door when the phone rang, and Zelda called her back.

"It's Emile," Zelda whispered, handing Amy the phone.

Emile announced that he was feeling much better and would be returning to work the following morning. His son, also a baker, was on vacation and would come in and help Emile for a few days.

"Are you sure you're up to it?" Amy asked.

"Felice is wringing her hands," Emile said, "but I am going—how do you say—stir-crazy in the house with this woman hovering over me. I want to be back in my kitchen. I will be there tomorrow morning."

"Emile is coming back to work," she told Zelda, grinning from ear to ear. Excitement bubbled up. The timing was perfect. With Rachel and Emile both returning the next day, she and Neil were free to do their thing. "Hot dog!" Laughing, she hurried out the door and made a beeline for the travel agency.

Two hours later, with a mug of coffee in her hand and the tickets in her pocket, Amy knocked loudly on Neil's door and went in.

He was zonked out, one hand flopped carelessly over his head, his chest bare above the sheet drawn to his waist. And a very nice chest it was. More than nice. Sexy. Enticing. Smoothly muscled and golden tan, it rose and fell slowly, begging to be touched. She saw the small circular scars, faint but unmistakable, where his buttons must have seared his skin when he was struck by lightning as a child. She had a powerful impulse to touch them, kiss them gently.

Her grip on the mug tightened, and she resisted the impulse.

The planes of his face, softened by sleep into a sensual boyishness and faintly blurred by the beginnings of a golden beard, beckoned to her fingers as well. As did the classic form of his nose, the full curve of his lower lip. She recalled the feel of those lips against hers, lips that were magically supple and tantalizing.

She'd never realized that his lashes were so long, so lush. But when his lids were open, those magnificent eyes were so magnetic and startlingly beautiful in color that she hadn't paid the proper attention to their frames.

Curiosity tugged her gaze to the sheet and the outline that it covered.

Was he naked beneath it?

She felt herself go warm at the notion and chastised herself for invading his privacy and staring at him in secret. She ought to back out right now and leave him to his rest.

But she was too excited to let him sleep. She shook him. "Neil, wake up! I have a surprise."

He opened his eyes and blinked those beautiful baby blues, then smiled. "I was dreaming about you," he said, his voice hoarse. "Come here." He reached for her.

She avoided his grasp. "Don't. I'll spill your coffee. Here. Sit up and drink it. I have something to tell you. Something wonderful!"

He grinned and took a sip from the mug. "Tell me. You look as if you're about to burst."

She laughed, barely able to keep from jumping with glee. "I am. I have everything worked out. Now you already know that Rachel is coming home tomorrow, but you don't know that Emile called and he's coming back to work tomorrow too. Isn't that great?"

He stilled. His smile died. "And that's great? That means that I'll be leaving for sure."

"Uh-huh. But so will I! I was a little concerned about going off and leaving Rachel to handle things by herself, but now I don't have to worry. Wait till you hear my plans." She yanked the envelope from her pocket and waved it. "In here I have two tickets to Las Vegas. Our plane leaves an hour after Rachel's lands so I can say hello and good-bye at the airport. And listen to this, the travel agent found us a deal. She reserved us a suite for two weeks at the brand-new Zodiac Hotel and Casino on the strip, and it was mere peanuts! And to top it off, we get a week's free rental on a luxury car. I told her that we'd take a Cadillac convertible. Isn't that great?"

A slow smile spread over his face. "Sounds good to me. Come here." He put down his mug and reached for her.

"Wait!" She backed away. "You haven't heard the rest of my plan."

"There's more?"

"Lots more. I've figured out how you can

get your own laboratory to do research, a way you can thumb your nose at those jerks who tossed you out."

"Love, I've told you that setting up a lab would cost a fortune."

"But with your abilities, we can make a fortune. Gambling. In Las Vegas." She laughed and did a little jig. "Isn't it great!"

He didn't say anything.

"Don't you understand? With your psychokinetic abilities and with a little practice, you can beat the crap table, the roulette wheel, and the slot machines. We'll make a bundle, enough for a fine laboratory."

He frowned. "It doesn't seem quite honest."

"*Honest?* You're kidding."

He shook his head. "It seems like taking unfair advantage."

"Oh, don't be silly. The casinos take unfair advantage of people every day to the tune of millions of dollars. It's called house odds." He still looked dubious. She grabbed his hand. "I have an idea. Come with me."

"May I put my pants on first?"

"Yes, but hurry up." She turned her back and tapped her foot while he pulled on a pair of jeans. As soon as she heard the zipper go up, she caught his hand and hustled him to the apartment upstairs.

Escape...
into Romance and embrace special savings.
Get 4 New Loveswept® Romances
for just $1.99 !
Plus FREE shipping and handling!
Get swept away by 4 New Loveswept Romances. Preview them risk-free—with no obligation and nothing to buy!
Keep them and Save $12.00! That's...
85% Off the cover price!
Get a FREE Gift!
To get your FREE personal lighted make-up case, peel off and affix this sticker inside!

Save 85% Off the Cover Price on 4 New *Loveswept* Romances—

and Get a Free Gift just for Previewing them for 15 Days Risk-Free!

Imagine two lovers wrapped in each other's arms—a twilight of loneliness giving way to a sunlit union. Imagine a world of whispered kisses and windswept nights, where hearts beat as one until dawn. If romance beats in your heart and a yearning stirs in your soul, then seize this moment and embrace *Loveswept!*

Let us introduce you to 4 new, breathtaking romances—**yours to preview and to lose yourself in for 15 days Risk-Free**. If you decide you don't want them, simply return the shipment and owe nothing. **Keep your introductory shipment and pay our low introductory price of just $1.99! You'll save $12.00—a sweeping 85% off the cover price! Plus no shipping and handling charges!** Now that's an introduction to get passionate about!

Then, about once a month, you'll get 4 thrilling Loveswept romances hot off the presses—*before they're in the bookstores*—and, from time to time, special editions of select *Loveswept* Romances. Each shipment will be billed at our low regular price, currently only $2.50* per book—a **savings of 29% off** the current cover price of $3.50. You'll always have 15 days to decide whether to keep any shipment at our low regular price—but **you are never obligated to keep any shipment**. You may cancel at any time by writing "cancel" across our invoice and returning the shipment to us, at our expense. So you see there is **no risk** and **no obligation** to buy anything, *ever!*

Treat Yourself with an Elegant Lighted Make-up Case—Yours Absolutely Free!

You'll always be ready for your next romantic rendezvous with our elegant Lighted Make-up Case—a lovely piece including an assortment of brushes for eye shadow, blush, and lip color. And with the lighted make-up mirror *you* can make sure he'll always see the passion in your eyes!

Keep the Lighted Make-up Case—yours absolutely FREE, whether or not you decide to keep your introductory shipment! So, to get your FREE Gift and your 15-Day Risk-Free preview, just peel off the Free Gift sticker on the front panel, affix it to the Order Form, and mail it today!

*(Plus shipping and handling, and sales tax in New York, and GST in Canada. Prices slightly higher in Canada.)

Save 85% off the Cover Price on
4 *Loveswept* Romances with this
Introductory Offer and Get
a *Free Gift* too!
no risk • no obligation • nothing to buy!

Get 4 Loveswept Romances for the Introductory Low Price of just $1.99!

Plus no shipping and handling charges!

Get 4 Loveswept books for the Introductory Low Price of just $1.99! And no shipping and handling charges!

Plus get a FREE Lighted Make-up Case!

You risk nothing—so act now!

"Where are we going?"

"To use the phone. I'm going to call Las Vegas. Get on the extension in Rachel's room."

She found the number for the Zodiac on their itinerary and dialed it. After being passed around among several people she ended up speaking with the chief of security.

"I have a question," she said. "If I have a friend who can influence the dice or the roulette wheel with the power of his mind, is it okay if we gamble there?"

The man roared with laughter. "God bless 'em, now I've heard it all. Tell him to come on. People have thought up all sorts of systems, and they're welcome to try them. There's no law against using your mind." He laughed again.

Amy walked into Rachel's room where Neil was hanging up the phone. "You heard."

Solemnly, he nodded.

"He thought I was nuts."

He nodded again.

A slow grin spread over her face.

An answering grin spread over his.

She threw herself into his arms, and he swung her around. "Las Vegas, here we come!"

EIGHT

The moment they stepped from the jetway, they were greeted by the clink of coins and the ding of bells from slot machines arranged in rows in the center of the waiting area.

"Welcome to Las Vegas," Amy said, grinning.

"You're excited about this, aren't you?" Neil asked.

"How could you tell?"

Neil smiled down at her adorable, dimpled face, so open and animated that her every thought and emotion was reflected there. He kissed her nose. "Because you've been bouncing around like a Mexican jumping bean for the past twenty-four hours. Sure you aren't on amphetamines?"

"I don't need speed. I get wired naturally."

He laughed. "Don't I know it. Come on. Let's get our bags."

In short order, they collected their luggage and picked up their rental car—a red Cadillac convertible. He got a kick out of how thrilled Amy was about that car. Since they'd gained two hours traveling west, it was still afternoon when they drove out of the agency, following the map they'd been given.

Only a short distance from the airport, a huge pyramid and Sphinx loomed from the palm-courted desert.

"Wow," she said. "That's the Luxor. It wasn't built when I was here before. And there's the Excalibur—that's the castle. And, oh, oh, that must be the MGM Grand. It's *huge*. But the lion doesn't look anything like it does on the TV ad."

He chuckled. "Poetic license."

"I'm sure that it's stunning at night. Everything about this place is stunning at night. It's a sea of flashing lights and neon. It's like being inside an electric kaleidoscope. And wait till you see Caesars Palace. The grounds alone will blow your mind. It looks like something from *Ben Hur*. Look, there it is! Oh, isn't it all fabulously exciting?"

"Fabulously."

She shot him a dirty look. "Are you making fun of me?"

He laughed. "Never. Is that our hotel?"

"No, that's The Mirage. Michael Jackson always stays there. And there's Treasure Island, and over there is the Valhalla. See the one with the Viking ship out in front? It's new, too, but ours is one of the newest in town." She checked the map. "We should be just on down . . . there. On the left. There it is. Ho-ly mo-ley. Look at that place."

"What's it supposed to be?"

"I don't know, but it looks like a cross between a Greek temple, an observatory, and the hanging gardens of Babylon. Interesting, wouldn't you say?"

"Definitely interesting," he replied, studying the place while stopped at a traffic light. Figuring for fountains and swimming pools alone, Neil was appalled at the amount of water the town must use frivolously. And in the desert. But not wanting to burst Amy's bubble, he kept silent. Besides, her enthusiasm was infectious. He was determined to ignore practicality and focus on having a good time. He wasn't sure that her cockeyed scheme would work, but at least they could have some fun before he had to devise some sort of career plan.

They turned into a drive lined with fountains, Olympic flames, and golden statues of rams, archers, and crabs.

"Oh, look, there's mine, the water carrier," she said, pointing to a statue. "What's your astrological sign?"

He chuckled. "I can't believe you asked me that. Surely you don't believe in all that rot."

"Why not? It's fun. Everything here is geared toward the zodiac. I'm an Aquarius, the water carrier. All the statues are symbolic of the signs. What's yours? I'll bet you're a Taurus or a Capricorn."

"Nope. I'm a Leo."

"The lion." She made a deep-throated growl, then laughed. "How revealing. You've been hiding some *very* interesting parts of yourself, Dr. Larkin."

The moment they stopped beneath the columned portico, they were approached by attendants wearing loose white pants and shirts decorated with a Greek key design and vaguely reminiscent of draped Grecian chitons. A young man whose name tag identified him as Dan, a Cancer, took their bags, while another, Chuck, a Libra, took care of parking the car.

They followed Dan inside, past more statues, flames, trailing greenery, and fountains. Straight ahead through more columns was the casino with its scores of game tables and hundreds, maybe thousands, of slot machines flashing and clicking and clinking. A party atmosphere of gaiety, laughter, conversation, and sudden shouts permeated the air and rose to the high-domed ceiling.

"Ho-ly mo-ley," Neil said, looking up at the vast ceiling. Painted like an indigo sky, it was filled with winking stars and the various constellations were outlined in glowing neon.

"I can't believe you said that." Amy giggled. "That's my line. Isn't it magnificently garish? Come on, let's register."

He shook his head in wonderment. "I feel like a country boy who's come to the big city."

They followed Dan to the registration desk, and while Amy stood fascinated with a giant aquarium, Neil took care of the arrangements with Cindy, a Virgo with a blond ponytail. There was a slight hitch, but Neil assured the flustered Cindy that they would manage.

Upstairs, Dan ushered them into an opulent suite, plush but not gaudy, and while Neil tipped the bellboy, Amy went exploring.

The living room was lovely, Amy thought, her bedroom was very nice, decorated predominantly in deep forest-green with lush velvet spreads on the double beds and with a variety of stylized ancient Greek and astrological accents —but the bathroom!

Talk about sumptuous. Done in white marble and green-and-rose-antiqued paper, it took her breath away. There was a sunken tub with gold dolphin faucets that was more of a spa than a bathtub. She could hardly wait to climb into it.

"Neil, come in here! You've got to see this."

He ambled in. "Very nice."

"Is yours this fancy?"

"Uhhhh, Amy, there was a bit of a snag with the suite. We'll have to share the bathroom."

She hesitated only a moment. "We can handle that. Where is the other bedroom? Is there a connecting door?" She looked around, but didn't see one.

"Uhhhh, that's the other part of it. There's only one bedroom. Two beds, but one bedroom. I suppose there was some sort of mixup with the reservation. I can sleep on the couch."

"Can't we get another room?"

He shook his head. "All filled up. A chiropractors' convention, I believe. Do you want to try another hotel?"

She considered his question very carefully. The idea of sharing space intimately with Neil was suddenly very titillating.

Too titillating.

Don't be silly, she told herself. They were adults. Hadn't they slept an entire night together in the same bed in New Orleans? Of course they had literally *slept*. Nothing had happened.

She could handle this.

Then she glanced up to find Neil's gaze on her.

His eyes were smoldering again.

Heat rose up from somewhere low, deep, and hidden inside her.

Every moment of every day that she and Neil spent together sparked more and more sexual awareness between them. A restless, dull ache in her body had become a perpetual companion.

Who would she be kidding? Their coming together was only a matter of time. She would be lying to herself if she claimed otherwise. Even if she wanted to. And she didn't.

They might as well save the price of another room.

"No," she answered, her voice a little breathless from the route her thoughts had taken, "we don't need to try another hotel. And you don't need to sleep on the couch. There are two beds here. We'll manage."

Was that her imagination or did his eyes smolder even more?

She suddenly felt very awkward. The silence in the room made it worse. Just because she admitted that they were headed for a sexual relationship didn't mean that she was quite comfortable with the idea yet.

She swung her arms and clapped her hands together. "Well," she said, clapping again, "why don't we go downstairs and look around? We can have a drink or something."

He chuckled. "Think we should unpack first?"

"Unpack. That's a great idea. We'll unpack." She started to grab one of her bags, but he stopped her and turned her to him.

"Amy, are you nervous?"

"Nervous? Me? Whatever gave you that idea? This tic in my eyelid is from a vitamin deficiency."

He laughed and hugged her. "Relax. I'm not going to jump your bones while you sleep."

"You're not? Oh shoot," she said, snapping her fingers.

He cocked an eyebrow wickedly. "Then again, perhaps I might."

Her temperature rose ten degrees.

It was definitely cooler downstairs in the casino. But the score or so people gathered around one of the crap tables were in a heated commotion. Amy drew her slim paperback book with tips on gambling from her shoulder bag and thumbed to the section on craps. While people were shouting, "Come! Don't come!"— which sounded a bit risqué to one unfamiliar with the terminology—and a dozen other things at once, she studied the book's drawing of the personnel positions and table layout.

As they peeked over the shoulders of the wild crowd bellied up to the table like lady fingers around a sponge cake, Amy whispered, "The guy sitting in the little niche with all the chips in front of him must be the boxman, and the fellows on either side are dealers." She pointed to the figure in the book. "The man across the table from the boxman, the one with the thing that looks like a putter, he must be the stickman. And the woman in yellow is the shooter."

"Coming out!" a dealer shouted midst a frenzy of arms and chips.

"Craps!"

"Snake-eyes!"

"Next shooter up. Place your bets."

"Coming out!"

"Four! Four is the point."

More flailing of bodies and chips and arms.

It was all going so fast and furiously that Amy couldn't keep up with anything.

"Well, what do you think?" she whispered to Neil.

"I think it moves too quickly and is too complicated for me to tackle—at least for the moment. It looked easy enough in that book, but we didn't factor in a boisterous crowd and such rapid action. And remember the crap table has a pair of dice, not just one. And they're considerably larger and heavier than a Monopoly die."

"I think you're right. Daunting, isn't it? We need to study it some more and come back when the crowd is sparser. Want to try the slots? We could start with the quarter ones."

He grinned. "You're having a fit to get at those one-armed bandits, aren't you?"

"Does it show? I love 'em."

"I could tell. Pick us out a couple of lucky ones."

Hand in hand they wandered among the rows and rows of slot machines where bells dinged and coins clinked into the metal troughs when a player hit a winning combination. She finally settled on an interesting-looking pair that were next to each other.

"I like the ones with cherries. I seem to do better on those. We'll need some change."

Neil signaled the change person, a young woman a tad too plump for the flowing, corseted chiton she wore. When Amy tried to pay for her coins, he shook his head and gave the woman a twenty for two rolls of quarters.

"My treat," he said, handing her the paper-wrapped cylinder.

"But this is just for fun," she said. "I'd rather use my own money." She grinned. "That way if I win, I won't feel guilty about keeping it. And if I lose, I won't feel guilty about squandering yours."

"Forget the guilt. I'll stake us to gambling money and expenses. I may be out of a job, but I'm not broke." He chuckled. "At least not yet. Just don't go crazy. How does this thing work?"

"Simple. You put the coins in here"—she pointed—"and either push this button or pull the handle, whichever suits your fancy. With these machines, it's better to put in three coins at a time. And if any of the combinations illustrated at the top come up on this line, you win. It's all computerized. Here, I'll show you."

She dumped her quarters into a paper cup, then put three coins in the slot and pushed the button. The four cylinders spun and one by one stopped. Nothing matched.

She tried again.

A cluster of cherries stopped on the left row.

Nothing else matched. Two quarters clunked into the metal bin. "See?"

"I see that you put a dollar and a half into the machine and got back fifty cents. Don't you even get a package of gum?"

"Oh, you!" She laughed and whacked him on the shoulder. "Try it. It's fun."

She turned back to feeding coins into the slot while Neil unwrapped his roll. She watched him from the corner of her eye as he put three coins in and pulled the handle.

His machine went crazy and started spitting out quarters like a stamping machine at the Denver Mint. "What happened?" he asked, watching the growing pile clinking into the bin.

"You won! You won a hundred dollars!" Bouncing in her seat and grinning, she pointed to the line. "See, they match." She clutched his arm. "My Lord, Neil, we're going to clean up. You could win the Megabucks jackpot. It's almost ten million dollars!"

"Uh, Amy—"

"Think of it! Ten million dollars!" She threw her arms around his neck and kissed his face in a hundred places. People were laughing and staring, but she didn't care.

"Uh, Amy . . ."

"What?"

He leaned close and whispered in her ear. "I didn't do anything. It was pure luck."

Her smile died. "You didn't . . . you know . . . ?"

He shook his head.

"Well, shoot! Try it again anyway. This time try"—she looked around furtively—"you know what."

They both continued to play, winning a little here and there, but their stash dwindled until Amy used all her coins and was snitching from Neil's winnings. He had played more slowly, eyes narrowed, watching the cylinders spin.

"Let's stop while we're ahead," he said finally, slapping his thighs. "I'm getting a headache. How about some dinner?"

"A headache?" She touched his temples. "Oh, Neil, I'm sorry. Yes, let's eat. Las Vegas has some of the finest food in the world. What sounds good?"

After a lovely dinner of grilled lamb chops and Greek salad in the Zenith Room they lingered over coffee and enjoyed the view of the night sky above the glass-domed restaurant. Amy noticed that he'd been awfully quiet during their meal.

"Do you still have a headache?" she asked.

"No. It's gone. But I don't think I'm going to be much good with the slot machines unless I get plain lucky. Certainly not without a great deal of practice. Maybe not even then. Sometimes I could get the first one, and occasionally I could influence the last one. I hit three a couple of times, but I think it was more random chance than anything else. With four cylinders spinning, I can't concentrate on all of them at once. And while they stop independently, there isn't enough time for me to refocus." He reached for her hand across the table. "Sorry."

Amy grinned. "Sort of reminds me of the lady with the spinning tassels in New Orleans, except in reverse. I admire her control even more now that I think about it." She patted his hand. "And hey, there's nothing to be sorry about. We're just getting our feet wet here. If the dancer in the Quarter could learn to do her trick with practice, maybe practice would help you too."

He looked down at his chest, then back up at her and said with a straight face, "No, I don't think I have the basic equipment for it. The pasties with the tassels wouldn't fit." A devilish gleam came in his eye. "But perhaps you could try it."

Amy burst into laughter. "Not likely. I'm so

poorly coordinated that I can barely walk and chew gum at the same time. And you know very well I was talking about practicing on the slots, not tassels. But forget them for now. I have a hunch about something. If you're up to it, we can try roulette."

"Wouldn't you rather take in a show?"

"Maybe later. Let's scout the roulette game."

Neil signed their check, and they went downstairs to wander through the casino area, looking for a roulette table that wasn't overrun with gamblers.

When they spotted a three-dollar table with only four players, she nudged him. "That looks about my speed. Let's get a few chips and play for fun while you get a feel for the situation. Remember that you have to bet at least three dollars on the inside numbers or the outside do-hickeys."

"Doohickeys?"

"Yeah. The odd/even, black/red, or the bunches."

"Ah, those doohickeys. I remember." He grinned and handed the dealer money to buy chips for each of them. The dealer slid a stack of orange chips toward Amy and a stack of purple ones toward Neil.

Amy tried to maneuver Neil close to the wheel so that he had a clear view of it, but a little old lady with white curls and a determined look on her face was firmly entrenched in the best vantage point. She had a hefty stockpile of pink chips in front of her, a drink with a pineapple slice and a tiny parasol in her left hand, and appeared to be dug in for the duration.

After several spins of the wheel, the orange chips soon disappeared completely, the purple chips were holding their own, and the pink pile grew considerably. A young guy with blue chips at the end of the table was pretty hot too.

"Want some more?" Neil asked when he saw that Amy's chips were depleted.

She shook her head. "I'll just watch for a while. You go ahead." She stepped back and sipped the diet cola she'd ordered from a passing cocktail waitress and began her favorite pastime—people watching.

A few steps away, a young woman, wearing obviously inexpensive clothes, caught her eye. Amy didn't need her social work degree to determine that the young blonde was extremely anxious. She alternately wrung her hands and chewed her nails as she watched the young man with the blue chips placing bets. Amy could have no more ignored a person in such severe distress than she could have kicked a wounded dog. She edged closer.

The blonde's nails were down to the quick, and as the man she was watching placed a large blue stack on even, the young woman turned her back and squeezed her eyes together. "I can't look," she murmured.

Amy watched the ball drop into a slot. "Twenty-eight," she told the woman. "He won."

Her face broke into a broad smile. "He did?"

Amy nodded.

"Oh, that's wonderful," she squealed. But when another stack of blue chips was pushed onto the red square, and an equal amount was distributed among several number combinations, the young woman grasped Amy's arm with one hand and clenched the other. She closed her eyes and said, "Tell me when it's over. I can't stand much more of this."

"Is he your husband?"

The woman nodded.

"If watching him play is so painful for you," Amy said, "why don't you go someplace else?"

"Oh, I couldn't. We have so much riding on this, you see. Carl is lucky, real lucky. He won this trip to Las Vegas that a radio station back home was giving away, and we just knew it was an omen."

With only an interested nod from Amy to encourage her, the young woman, named Melissa Rowen she discovered, had soon told Amy the most intimate details of her life. It wasn't an unusual situation; virtual strangers were always telling Amy the most intimate details of their lives. They homed in on her as if she wore a signaling device.

Carl and Melissa had a two-year-old daughter named Stacy who needed hip surgery that cost thirty-two thousand dollars more than would be covered by Carl's health insurance from the discount store where he worked selling small appliances.

"So when he won the trip last Friday," Melissa said, "we knew it was an omen. We left Stacy with my mother and cashed Carl's paycheck to use as a stake."

"And are you winning?"

Melissa nodded. "Sixteen thousand dollars so far. Most of it's upstairs in the safe in the room. I hope he quits for the night pretty soon. My nerves can't take much more. By the time a week's up, I'll be a wreck."

"I understand." Amy patted her arm. "Have you considered going to some of the agencies in the town where you live? I'm sure that you could get some help to defray the cost of Stacy's surgery."

Melissa shook her head. "Carl's real proud," she said. "He won't accept charity."

Amy started to argue, but changed her mind when she saw the set of Melissa's lips. In any case, the conversation ended when Neil turned from the table, looking for her. "Good luck," she said to Melissa before joining him.

"Run into someone you know?" he asked.

"No." She explained the young couple's situation to him.

"I hope Carl has better luck than I did."

"You lost?"

"No," he said, handing her a small stack of five-dollar chips, "but I didn't exactly set the world on fire either." He yawned. "I don't know about you, but I'm still on New Orleans time and ready for bed. Want to call it a night?"

His yawn was contagious, and she yawned as well. After he mentioned it, she realized that she *was* tired. Exhausted, in fact. Neither she nor Neil had a decent night's rest since Emile had been injured. How nice it would be to snuggle in the covers and sleep until noon. How enticing the notion of a soft bed was.

Bed.

Beds.

Two beds. In the same room.

Oh, dear.

She blinked her eyes wide open and pasted a perky smile on her face. "Call it a night? Me? Heavens no. Why I'm just getting my second wind. How about another go at the slot machines?"

For a moment Neil didn't say anything. He simply stared at her while she fidgeted. Then faint amusement played at his lips.

"Why are you staring at me?" she asked. "Do I have poppy seeds in my teeth or something?"

The signs of amusement blossomed into a chuckle. "This time it's *your* nose that's growing. I can see that you're almost dead on your feet. You're nervous about going upstairs and sharing a bedroom with me, aren't you?"

"*Me?* Certainly not. How silly. I'm simply not sleepy." She clenched her molars to keep from yawning again.

He kissed her nose. "Come on upstairs. I'll sleep on the couch." He steered her to the elevators.

"There is absolutely no need for you to be uncomfortable. There are two perfectly good beds. We are adults; we can handle this in a sensible fashion."

They rode up in the car alone. She didn't

speak; her eyes were glued to the indicator as the numbers flashed closer and closer to the ninth floor.

By the time the door whooshed open, her palms were dripping.

NINE

When the door to their suite swung open, she felt as jittery as a virgin on her wedding night. And for no earthly reason. She was neither virgin nor bride. But neither had she ever shared such close quarters with a man before—not even with her ex-fiancé. And certainly not one who made her feel the way Neil Larkin did. She wasn't afraid that he'd "jump her bones." She was more afraid that she'd jump his—and be rejected. Not rejected sexually—she could feel the chemistry between them—but rejected emotionally.

It had happened before. And with a man almost, but not quite, as handsome as Neil. She was cursed with ordinary, girl-next-door looks; though she could appear reasonably attractive when she made special efforts, she wasn't in the same league as beautiful people like Neil . . . or Michael, her ex-fiancé. She hadn't missed the speculative scrutiny people made of Neil and her as a couple. They were the same kind of assessments she used to get when she was with Michael. The How-did-someone-like-you-snag-a-hunk-like-him? look.

"You want the bathroom first?"

Neil's question startled her from her reverie. "Uh, no. You go first. You're tired, and I'd like a leisurely soak in that glorious tub."

He cupped her cheek and kissed her briefly. "I won't take long."

Her heart went into overdrive. She tried to calm herself while he took his shaving kit and a couple of other items and disappeared into the bathroom.

She dithered as she paced the floor, dithered as she gathered her belongings for the bathroom. She was still dithering when he came out, sexy as a movie star, wearing a terry hotel robe and toweling his damp hair.

"It's all yours. Just don't stay until you turn into a prune," he said, winking.

Trying to act blasé, she smiled, grabbed her small case and went through the door he'd just exited. It didn't help that his smell lingered in the marble room. She took a deep breath, and all sorts of erotic images filled her mind.

Her anxiety level went off the scale.

Stop it! she told herself as she ran water into the enormous tub.

She was blowing this situation all out of proportion. So Neil was a hunk. So she was outrageously attracted to him. So the constant heat she felt could boil new potatoes. So what? It wasn't as if they were in love. They hadn't made impassioned commitments or professions of undying devotion. She hadn't even know him that long.

Thinking about Michael and his defection for a former Miss Texas had stirred up this hornet's nest in her head. And she hadn't thought about Michael in months and months.

When the tub had filled, she sprinkled scent into the water, climbed in, and turned on the jets.

Ahhhh, heaven.

Of course she'd thought about Michael a lot after he'd broken their engagement. Well, he hadn't technically broken their engagement; she had. But only after he'd shown up at a couple of major events escorting Miss T, and she'd had no choice but to toss his ring in his face. She always figured that he'd publicly humiliated her to get his ring back, so that she would play the scene exactly as she had. The big rock, rather ostentatious now that she thought about it, had

set him back a bundle. He liked show. The
good life. The fast buck in the fast lane. He
didn't have the sort of admirable dedication to
bettering the world that Neil did with his cancer research.

Neil was a man of high principles and altru-
ism, a true humanitarian. That was why she was
so attracted to him. Well . . . that and his
body.

She was well rid of Michael, the shallow
jerk. She knew that. And she couldn't for the
life of her understand how they'd gotten together in the first place.

Yes, she could. Sexual attraction. They were
compatible in bed. For a while. As long as she
was submissive and adoring, as long as she de-
manded nothing for herself. And their breakup
had devastated her. For a while. She'd recovered. But she'd been celibate during the three
years since.

Maybe that's why her libido was in such an
uproar now.

Yes, that was it. Neil Larkin was a darned
sexy man, and she was a warm-blooded woman.
She was ripe. No big deal. They could have a
lovely romp with no strings attached.

And from the signals he'd given out, she had
a strong hunch that Neil would be delighted if
she took the initiative.

That's exactly what she was going to do. She was going to put on a skimpy nightie, dab provocative perfume between her breasts, and slip between his sheets.

Then why was she still sitting in the tub with her fingers and toes shriveling?

After another fifteen minutes of positive self-talk, she got out and dried herself off. She spent another fifteen brushing her hair, dabbing perfume, applying lip gloss, and deciding which of her rather modest nighties looked the skimpiest.

The moment of truth had arrived. She could delay no longer. Taking a deep, fortifying breath, she opened the bathroom door and walked slowly into the bedroom.

Her whole body zinged with anticipation. Her pulse pounded. Her skin tingled. Her breasts were swollen, her nipples sensitive against the fabric of her gown. Even the carpet seemed to turn her bare feet into an erogenous zone.

Hips swaying slightly, she padded slowly to the bed where the dim lamp outlined his masculine form beneath the sheets.

"Neil," she murmured.

He didn't move.

She drew closer.

"Neil," she whispered, touching his bare shoulder lightly.

Nothing.

His eyes were closed, his breathing measured.

She shook him.

Nothing. He was out like a light.

"Well, damn!" she muttered, marching to her bed and jerking back the covers. "Damn and double damn!"

Neil stood beside Amy's bed and watched her sleep. She looked so adorable with her hair all tumbled, so sexy with her lips swollen and slightly parted, so enticing with the tiny strap fallen from her bare shoulder that it took a mammoth amount of control to keep him from stripping off his clothes and climbing in beside her. That was why he'd escaped downstairs for an early breakfast and why he'd tentatively agreed to a golf game with some guys he'd met in the coffee shop.

With his mind he lifted a tousled curl that had fallen across her cheek and stroked it. He could almost, but not quite, feel its silkiness. God, how he longed to tangle both hands in it and feel it for real. He shoved his hands into his pockets to resist the temptation.

"Amy," he whispered.

"Hmmmm?" She shifted positions and kicked a foot from under the covers.

"How long do you want to sleep?"

"Noon," she mumbled into her pillow, never opening her eyes.

He couldn't seem to take his eyes from her foot and ankle. Nor could he harness his recalcitrant mind as it slowly pushed the sheet up until a lovely expanse of leg was bared to midthigh. Long, perfectly curved, it was part of the pair that haunted his dreams. He touched her flesh with his thoughts, but it didn't satisfy him. He wanted to feel the warmth of her skin against his. Taking one hand from his pocket, he hesitated, then allowed his fingertips to graze the warm smoothness of her calf only a moment, then drew back.

He'd promised himself—and her—that he wouldn't take advantage of the situation, but damn it was difficult. He'd awakened early that morning and lain in bed listening to her breathe, knowing that the woman he ached for was only a few steps away. He'd grown more restless and harder by the minute until he forced himself to dress and escape to the coffee shop.

Standing here now wasn't any easier. Maybe

nine holes of golf would help. He jotted a quick note for her and left.

Amy came awake slowly. Stretching, she rolled over and glanced at her travel clock. Nine-thirty. Holy moley! She sat up and checked Neil's bed. It was mussed but empty. She fell back on the pillow and snuggled for a few minutes, taking her time waking up.

Even as tired as she'd been, Amy had almost not fallen asleep the night before. She'd been too revved up. Listening to Neil breathe and knowing that he was only a few feet away didn't help her condition any. Several times she had seriously considered making that short trip to his bed and awakening him, but she wasn't quite that bold.

Just thinking about Neil again made her tingle all over. And that familiar low pulsation was back. Maybe now that he was rested . . . maybe. . . . She smiled and stretched, her body sensitive to the rasp of the sheets against her skin. If it took bold, she'd be bold. She'd be seductive. She'd be a stalking tigress.

But first she had to find him.

Wondering where he was, she sat up, called out his name, and looked around. That's when

she noticed the note propped against the tele-
phone.

Golf? He'd gone to play *golf?* Here she was
in the throes of sexual yearning that had her
about to climb the walls, and he'd gone to play
golf.

Thoroughly angry, she threw off the covers
and stomped to the bathroom. She almost
brushed the enamel off her teeth while she muttered vile deprecations related to Neil and his
ancestry.

After room service delivered coffee and a
croissant—not nearly as good as the ones she
and Neil made—she performed her morning
routine, including two layers of mascara on her
eyelashes. She dressed quickly in khaki slacks
and a red cotton sweater and stowed a few essentials in a waist pack.

She almost left without writing him a note,
but reneged and scribbled a short one telling
him that she was off to hit the slots and would
meet him at the Dolphin Pool at The Mirage
around noon. *If* he was back from playing golf
by then, of course. It was a shame sarcasm
didn't translate well into the written word. The
acid would have burned a hole in the page.

In the casino, she located a machine with
cherries and claimed the stool in front of it.
When she went through a roll of quarters in

record time, she decided to wash off the gray gunk on her fingers that was the bane of slot players, and stroll on down to The Mirage.

The weather outside was so glorious that her pique quickly evaporated. She wandered around leisurely, stopping to browse in souvenir shops and laugh at some of the unbelievably tacky items for sale. She bought a few postcards and examined a display of dice.

When an idea struck her, she asked the proprietor, "Are these regulation size? I mean, are these like the ones they use at the casino crap tables?"

After he assured her that they were, she bought two sets and stashed them in her zippered pack along with the postcards. At a concession next door, she bought a banana ice cream on a stick and walked toward the Viking ship moored in a small pit of water in front of the new Valhalla Hotel.

A small crowd was gathering in front of the stone wall stretched along the street side. The display, artfully decorated to depict a stone cliff along the ocean, reminded her a bit of a seal habitat at the zoo—except for the fierce-prowed Viking ship, of course. Several young men, dressed in short, furry garbs and wearing horned helmets were milling around the deck of the ship. Assuming that they were about to do some kind of performance, Amy pushed her sunglasses up on her nose and joined the crowd at the railing.

Just as she bent her head sideways to lick a dribble from her banana stick, she spotted a little boy about four scaling the stone wall at the far end of the setting. She pointed and shouted at the same time that a cannon exploded and all hell broke loose on the Viking ship. Nobody heard her.

Keeping her eyes on the child's precarious position, she kept yelling and tried to elbow her way through the boisterous crowd. No one paid any attention, and the press of people made it almost impossible to move. Before she could get to him, the boy slipped and plunged into the water in the far corner of the rocky cliff.

Panic shot adrenaline into her. She scrambled up the wall and over the railing, yelling to the Vikings and pointing to where the boy went under.

They only laughed and brandished their rubber swords.

Curious about the noise and crowd in front of Valhalla, Neil stopped to look. A flash of red atop the fence caught his eye. A woman. Waving her arms and screaming like a banshee.

My God, it was *Amy*!

The realization came at the same instant she held her nose and jumped.

His heart pounding, he plunged through the crowd to the railing. Seconds after he barreled into the pandemonium that had broken out, he looked down to see her surface with a child wrapped around her neck like a monkey. Neil was about to climb over after her when a kid in a fur outfit slid down a rope and grabbed them. A woman in the crowd screamed, "Timmy!" hysterically as two other Norsemen plunged into the water.

They soon had everybody out.

By the time Neil made his way behind the staging area, both Amy and the child were wrapped in blankets and ringed by security and hotel personnel. The woman who had screamed and a man who looked as if he were about to arrived close on his heels.

A siren wailed nearby.

Neil tried to push his way to Amy, but a burly guard ordered him to stand back.

No way in hell.

"I'm with the woman," Neil said.

"If you'll just wait here, sir," the guard said. "An ambulance is on its way."

"I'm a doctor," Neil added.

The magic words got him through. Of

course as a Ph.D., he didn't know a damned thing about treating any sort of injury beyond using basic first-aid techniques. Thankfully there were a couple of other doctors around, a pediatrician from Omaha and a urologist from San Francisco. And the paramedics arrived about the time he took Amy into his arms.

She was shivering like a leaf in a storm. She clung to him and, with her teeth chattering, said, "Oh, Neil, I've never been so glad to see anyone in my life. Is the little boy okay?"

"I think so. Are you hurt?"

"No, I'm okay, except for being very wet and a little shaky."

"What happened?"

"My lifesaver course just kicked in automatically." She tried as best she could to explain, but the area was mass confusion with hotel personnel, medical personnel, and curious onlookers crowding around.

After she refused to go to the hospital, the paramedics pronounced Amy fit but suggested that she consider getting some antibiotics to counteract any problems with water she may have swallowed. The urologist obligingly wrote her a prescription.

The child seemed okay as well. In fact he seemed to think the whole episode was neat, but his parents and all the hotel VIPs insisted on his going to the emergency room to be checked out.

One of those same VIPs bowed and scraped to Amy and, after securing her name and her hotel, snapped his fingers and a white limo arrived to drive them the few blocks to the Zodiac.

"Let me carry you," Neil said as they exited the limo.

She laughed. "We tried that once before, remember?"

"Yeah, but I'm sober this time."

"I'll walk, but thanks anyhow."

With Amy still wrapped in a blanket and trailing water, Neil hung on tightly to her as they darted through the lobby to the elevators.

As soon as they were inside their suite, she said, "I'll be okay once I've washed my hair and had a warm bath."

"Want me to help?"

"Your timing is lousy, Neil Larkin. I'll manage alone. How was your golf game?"

"Boring. I kept wishing I was with you." He led her to the bathroom. "Now get those wet clothes off and get into the tub."

Her shakes disappeared after about ten minutes of being massaged by warm water. After another five, she was back to normal. With her hair once again clean and fluffy, her makeup reapplied, Amy dressed in a comfortable print skirt and a purple top, then went into the living room.

Neil sat on the couch, and an enormous arrangement of red roses sat on the coffee table in front of him. He looked up at her and grinned.

"How does it feel to be a heroine?"

She shrugged. "I don't know. I've never asked one."

He laughed. "You're the heroine. And a very popular lady around here right now. We've had a parade of people through here." He held up a key. "This is for our new lodgings—one of the penthouse suites—compliments of the management, as are the roses. A bevy of maids and bellboys will be along at your convenience to move us."

"You're kidding."

"Nope. Anything your heart desires is compliments of the management."

"I wonder if they could rustle up a Reuben sandwich and some potato chips? I'm starving."

He waved a white envelope. "Food and drink at any of the major hotels in town is compliments of the Valhalla. But lunch will be served shortly in our new suite." He waved another envelope. "I understand that this is a hefty gift certificate to any of the shops in Caesars Palace for a new outfit to replace the one you ruined."

Her eyes widened. "Ho-ly mo-ley."

He laughed. "Exactly." He rose and offered his arm. "Shall we check out the new digs?"

"Sure. Let me get my purse. Oh . . . and I bought something for you today."

"For me?"

"Well, for us. Some regulation dice. We can practice."

Amy salvaged what she could from her wet waist pack. The postcards were a lost cause, but the dice fared fine in their cellophane wrapper as did her lipstick. Her wallet and its contents were damp, but they would dry. She wrapped the damp things in a hand towel and stuffed them in her shoulder bag, then went to join Neil.

He offered his arm again. "Our lunch is waiting for us."

A few minutes later, he unlocked the door to their new suite and Amy stepped inside. Her eyes grew wide with wonderment. "Ho-ly mo-ley. You could hold a bowling tournament in here. Is that an echo I hear?"

A waiter, who stood beside a table for eight but set for two with wineglasses and silver dome covers, nodded. "I'll serve your lunch when you're ready."

"Great. Just let me look around first."

Feeling like a hayseed, she wandered down the columned hallway to the living area. The floors were marble with beautifully loomed area rugs in the several seating areas. It even had a baby grand piano.

The huge room had windows from floor to ceiling on three sides and afforded a magnificent panorama. In its center was an ornate freestanding fireplace with a circular hood. She expected to see a bevy of Greek maidens come tripping in at any moment pouring wine from ewers and making sacrifices on the fireplace altar to Zeus and the other gods on Olympus.

"Nice, huh?" Neil said.

"It's beyond nice. It's awesome. And it's *free?*"

"That's what the man said. And it has three bedrooms and three baths."

"*Three?*"

"Three."

Rats! Amy thought. Now they would have separate bedrooms. She'd never get up the nerve to jump his bones in this place.

TEN

"Which do you think we should try?" Amy asked Neil as they strolled through the sky-domed casino at the Zodiac.

"Roulette, I think. I'm still not very reliable with two dice. A single ball is easier, and I think our system might work to our advantage."

Part of the system Neil referred to was simple enough. They had decided to find a table where Amy could sit next to the wheel and play. Neil wouldn't play but would stand behind and slightly to one side of her so that he would have full view of the wheel and the spinning ball.

The rest of the system was more complicated, involving the position of the wheel numbers, which weren't consecutive but were mixed up, and the layout of the betting area. Neil had come up with the combinations that would work to their advantage if he couldn't get the ball in the exact slot, but made it fall into one of the slots on either side.

"For example," he'd explained patiently as he pointed out the illustrations in the book they had, "say we select six as the target."

Remembering their Monopoly game, she grinned. "Let's do. Six is a lucky number."

"We'll have to change numbers, but we can start with six. It seems to be unique. Notice that the slots on either side of it are eighteen and twenty-one. And on the betting layout, eighteen and twenty-one are adjoining. So let's say you place a five-dollar bet on six and I can control it, you'll win at thirty-five to one. In other words, you'll win—"

"A hundred and seventy-five dollars."

"Exactly. But if my control is a little off, and the ball lands in slot eighteen or twenty-one—"

"I lose five dollars."

"Correct. But we can create insurance by placing another five-dollar bet, putting it on the line between eighteen and twenty-one and splitting it. If the ball lands on either of them, you'll win at seventeen to one."

She did some quick mental arithmetic. "And I'll win eighty-five dollars."

"Minus the five you lost on six would be eighty dollars."

"Hey, that's great! Or I can put five dollars on all of them. And if I bet ten dollars and you hit six, eighteen, or twenty-one, I'll win three hundred and fifty dollars minus ten. Or if I bet a hundred—"

"Whoa!" He laughed. "Let's not get carried away just yet. We've got to try it first. It's going to take some practice, and it may not work. Let's be conservative at first."

"It'll work. I just know it. I feel it in my bones. We're going to win tons and tons of money, and you can have your lab. You'll see." Excited at the prospect, she studied the drawings in the book. "Are all the numbers like the six? I mean, can we just pick one and split a second bet?"

"Unfortunately, no. But if this illustration is accurate, the nine is close, except you have to split your bets on the corner of four numbers to include the numbers adjacent to nine on the wheel. The odds drop to eight to one, so you can clear thirty dollars."

"Or I can just bet the two numbers adjacent." When he frowned, she said, "I know, I know. We'll start conservatively. Anyhow, I like the six idea better," she said. "It's easier to remember."

"So do I, but we'll have to mix them up if I start hitting. And you'll need to place a bet or two at random to keep things from looking suspicious."

They'd discussed strategy for the better part of the afternoon, and they'd decided to try their system that evening.

Now the hour of truth had come.

Amy was extremely nervous as they approached a table that looked like an ideal spot. Only two players occupied stools at the end away from the wheel. She wiped her damp palms on her skirt. When Neil handed two fifty-dollar bills to the dealer and asked for five-dollar chips, she grew more nervous. Seeing the cash made the whole thing suddenly very real.

Neil squeezed her shoulder and smiled. "You play. I think I'll just watch." He nipped her earlobe and whispered, "Let's go get 'em, tiger." Then he growled. He actually growled.

She was so discombobulated by his bit of suggestive play, that she almost forgot to place her bet. She had only time to put a chip on six when the dealer said, "No more bets, please."

Her heart in her throat, she watched the ball as it slowed, dropped, bounced, then dropped into slot eighteen. Stricken, she glanced at Neil. He only winked and squeezed her shoulder.

Turning back to the table, she focused her mind on the business at hand.

"I'm going to try six again," she said to no

one in particular. "It's my lucky number." She plunked a chip on six, one on eighteen, and a third on twenty-one.

The ball was spun.

"No more bets, please. No more bets."

Fingers crossed on both hands, breath held, she watched the little white ball spin round and round.

It bounced in and out of three slots before it came to rest with a clacking sound.

Six.

"Whoopee!" she yelled, throwing her arms into the air. She jumped up and down and hugged Neil. "I won! I won!"

He laughed. "You sure did. Good for you." In her ear, he whispered, "Try the nine combination."

She sat back down and savored the big stacks of chips she'd won. Feeling reckless, she put five chips on nine and five on the corner combination bet. For the heck of it, she put one on six.

Round and round the ball went.

Nine!

Amy almost went into cardiac arrest. She hung on to the table edge for support. Her eyes bugged out when she saw the number of chips the dealer shoved across the table to her. She didn't dare look at Neil. She put a stack of ten chips on six, and ten on both eighteen and twenty-one.

"There's a hundred-dollar limit on this table," the dealer said.

When Amy looked at him blankly, he explained, "Your inside bets can't total more than a hundred dollars."

She glanced at Neil. He shrugged. She removed the stack from eighteen.

Round and round the ball went.

She closed her eyes.

When it clacked into the slot and was still, she opened them. A couple of people yelled.

Twenty-one.

All the blood drained from her face as the dealer shoved one thousand, seven-hundred and fifty dollars to her in fifty- and twenty-five-dollar chips.

She looked around. A small crowd had gathered behind her, and Neil looked like the cat who'd been in the cream.

She picked up two fifty-dollar chips and plunked them on a square. "A hundred on my lucky six."

Round and round the ball spun again.

It dropped dead on six.

A cheer went up behind her.

Feeling decidedly green at the obscene amount of money being shoved at her, she turned to Neil and said, "Cash me in. I'm going to be sick." She pushed through the crowd and fled to the ladies' room.

When she came out, Neil was waiting for her, a concerned look on his face. "Are you okay?"

She took a deep breath and nodded. "Can we go somewhere quiet and have a drink? I need a ginger ale or something."

He steered her toward the lounge, and they found a secluded corner. "Are you sure you're okay?"

"I will be in a few minutes. Just give me a little while to get myself together."

He ordered two ginger ales from the cocktail waitress and didn't say a word until their drinks were delivered and Amy had taken a big swallow of hers.

"How much did we win?" she asked.

He emptied his jacket pockets which were bulging with hundred-dollar chips and arranged them on the table in stacks of ten. "I tipped the dealer with a fifty- and a twenty-five-dollar chip."

"There are six stacks of hundred-dollar chips there."

"Yep. With two left over." He fanned the two extras between his fingers.

"That's over six *thousand* dollars."

"Yep."

"Ho-ly cow."

"Exactly."

She clutched his arm. "Do you know what this means?"

A slow grin spread over his face. "It means, my little tiger, that we're going to clean up."

"Ho-ly cow."

He laughed. "Want to have some dinner or you want to give it another go at a table with higher stakes?"

"Right now, I couldn't eat a bite."

By midnight, Neil's pockets were bulging with thousand-dollar chips, and they had attracted a growing crowd around the roulette table. According to plan, she bet three random numbers each time, and with only a couple of exceptions, each time one of her numbers won.

Amy's stomach had held up better during the second assault, but now it growled. Loudly. "Let's stop," she whispered to Neil. "All these people make me nervous. And I'm hungry."

He nodded. "First let's change these chips into something more portable."

At the cashier, they deposited most of the winnings into an account in both their names and kept out a few thousand for playing money.

They ate lobster and drank champagne in the Zenith Room—compliments of the management. By the time Amy had finished her *crème brûlée* and a third glass of champagne, she was decidedly mellow.

"I could get used to all this," she said.

He grinned. "Me too. Heady, isn't it?"

Propping her elbows on the table, she cupped the wine flute in both hands and smiled at Neil. "We make a good team, you know that?"

"A darned good team." He smiled and ran his finger down her outer arm from wrist to elbow, then back again. Chill bumps popped up along the path. "Did you enjoy yourself at the tables tonight?"

"Winning thousands of dollars? What's not to enjoy? How about you? Did you have fun?"

He cocked his head and thought for a minute. A lopsided grin etched a dimple in one cheek. "Yeah. Yeah, I did. It was almost as much fun as playing Monopoly with you."

"We didn't exactly play Monopoly. We— Oh," she said, remembering the game. "What part did you like best?"

"The part where I kissed you." His gaze

went to her lips, and she licked them. "Want to play the game again?" His drawl was so blatantly seductive that she felt her vertebrae begin to disintegrate.

"I didn't bring the set along. But I know where there are some dice."

"Where?"

"Upstairs."

"Let's go."

They didn't wait to find the dice. The moment the door closed behind them, Neil wrapped his arms around her, uttered a feral sound, and covered her mouth with his. She responded with all the hunger that had been building in her for days.

Crowding her against the wall, he pressed his lower body close to hers. She could feel his hardness, and it sent her into orbit. Lips moist, tongues urgent, they kissed with a heated fervor that turned her into a wild thing. Her hands were all over him; she wanted to climb up his body.

"My God, woman," he said, his breath hot and ragged next to her ear, "what are you doing to me?"

"What am I doing to you? Dear Lord, what

are you doing to me? I feel like I'm about to explode."

She wanted to growl, strip him naked, and take little bites out of him. Rubbing her hands over his torso, she slid them higher and pushed his jacket down his shoulders. He shrugged out of it, and it dropped to the floor in a heap. His fingers fumbled for the buttons of her top, and he cursed when they ended with the placket.

"I want to touch you," he murmured against her throat as he alternately licked and nipped the skin there. "I want to taste you all over." He switched his assault to the ribbed bottom of her shirt, pushing it up until his palm could cup her breast.

"I want to touch you too. And taste you." With her mouth devouring his and one leg wrapped around his thighs, she worked feverishly at the buttons of his shirt while he unclasped her bra. When her fingers muddled the job on his shirt, she ripped the opening apart and sent buttons flying.

Her behavior sent him into a frenzy of kissing, moaning, rubbing, touching. "Oh, God, I want you." He shoved her bra aside and bent to take a nipple and suck it deeply into his mouth.

His action shot a painful jolt of need from her breast to her toes, ignited her senses until she felt like a blast furnace. "I want you too.

Oh, Neil, I want you so badly that I'm about to die."

Grabbing her hand, he pulled her down the hallway and into the first bedroom they came to, a trail of clothes littering the floor behind them, others half on and half off.

He stopped beside the bed and jerked back the cover. Only a distant hall lamp and the flashing neon kaleidoscope beyond the wide expanse of glass windows illuminated the room. His light eyes shining in the dim glow, he touched her cheek briefly, then took off his pants and fell onto the mattress, bringing her sprawling over him.

Between desperate kisses, the rest of their clothing was cast aside until they lay skin to skin. He rubbed his face in the valley of her breasts, then sank his mouth into the softness of her belly. He thrust his tongue into the indentation of her navel while she dug her fingers into the hard muscle of his shoulders and back.

He nipped and licked and kissed every surface, every fold, every hidden spot on her torso, murmuring love words and praises as he moved. When she hooked her bent leg over his taut hips, his fingers explored more wet, hidden folds, and his mouth plundered the aching fullness of her breasts with such inflaming adeptness that she thought she would go mad.

"Neil, please, I can't stand anymore." She tugged at his hips to bring him into the cradle of her thighs.

"Wait, love, wait."

She groaned as he pulled away momentarily, but soon he was back, rolling on protection as he knelt beside her. She couldn't drag her eyes from him. Pale hair and skin all of a color in the dimness, he looked like a perfectly sculpted Apollo in magnificent tumescence. But she touched him, and he was warm.

And he smelled of man and desire.

She opened her arms and waited.

Though their craving for each other still infused the air with barely contained electricity, their earlier roughness turned to a different dance.

His tongue on her breast was slow and tender. His splayed hand as he slid it up her leg from ankle to groin was an intensely soft caress. His gaze glistened so exquisitely sweet that tears sprang to her eyes when he smoothed her bangs from her forehead and whispered, "Amy. My Amy."

His hardness nudged against her gently, and she offered herself to him. He entered slowly as if savoring each millimeter he penetrated, as if she were porcelain threatening to shatter beneath him.

"I won't break," she said.

"But you're so tight. I don't want to hurt you."

"You won't hurt me."

She felt his muscles trembling against her fingers, and wanted to recapture the fierceness that had begun their encounter. His maddening, controlled slowness roused her hunger, heightened her impatience.

With a low growl, she raked his back with her nails and twining her legs around him, roughly pulled him downward as she thrust upward, deeply impaling herself on his hardness and demanding a vigorous response.

His control snapped. Wanton wildness drove them. They moved and strove in primitive abandon, writhing, lashing, driving, thrusting with hips and tongues until they glowed with sensual burning, and the scent of hot sex radiated out from them to fill the room.

He rolled to his back, and she rode him, reveling in erotic heat and vigorous maneuvers as he kneaded her breasts. "You're burning me up," he groaned.

"Welcome to the club," she gasped.

With a deft twist, she was again on her back with him thrusting deeply and making guttural sounds as she writhed and strove under him.

Deep, undulating waves of sensation began

rolling upward from her toenails and downward from her scalp. They crashed together in her womb, engulfing her, sending her into paralyzing spasms that bowed her back off the mattress and curled her fingers and toes.

Her climax set him off, and he exploded with a shout and a deep throbbing inside her.

For several moments they lay there, his weight tempered by his forearms. His breathing was ragged, as was hers. Drops of his sweat fell on her face and joined with the dampness of her own.

When she could speak, she said very softly, "Ho-ly mo-ley."

He chuckled. "Exactly."

After another few moments, he rolled to his side and gathered her close. He didn't say anything for what seemed like a week.

Wasn't this the part where both partners declared how good it was for them? She waited for his comment.

None came.

She didn't want to be the first one to say anything.

Waiting, she grew nervous. Then more nervous. Had she disappointed him? Had she been too bold? She'd never acted like a wild woman in bed before. But she'd never felt like a wild woman before. Neil had pushed buttons and transformed her into a person she didn't recognize. What if he was turned off by her wanton behavior? What if he thought she was some kind of oversexed hussy?

Growing more anxious with each passing second, she finally said, "No one has ever, *ever* made love to me like that before."

He groaned and flopped back flat on the bed. "Oh, God, I knew it. I was afraid of that. I blew it. I hurt you. Oh, Amy love, I'm sorry. I'm so sorry." He brushed her damp bangs back and blotted her face gently with a corner of the sheet.

She raised up and looked at him as if he were crazy. "Sorry? Why on earth would you be sorry? I thought it was fantastic."

"You did?"

"Sure. I mean, I may have gotten a little too turned on there and acted like a hussy, but you do strange things to my libido, Dr. Larkin. I'm not usually so . . . so sexually uninhibited."

"You're not?"

"Uh-uh." She sat up on her knees and rubbed her hands over his smooth chest. "Something about you just rang my bell, and I went berserk."

She could see the white flash of his teeth. "Well, you rang mine for damned sure."

She smiled smugly. "I did?"

He pulled her into his arms. "You did. I usually have more control, but with you around, I've given it up for a lost cause. I stay aroused most of the time."

"You do?"

"Yep."

She walked her fingers up his chest, then touched his lower lip. "Do you think it's a by-product of this place? Las Vegas, I mean. It's a seductive town, and winning all that money was a real turn-on."

He shook his head. "Not for me. I felt this way in New Orleans. The first night I met you. I had a hunch that things could be potent between us. Spontaneous combustion, I think I said."

She snuggled in the crook of his shoulder. "You were right about that." She yawned. "Is this your bedroom?"

He kissed her forehead. "It's ours now. Sleepy?"

She nodded and yawned again. "My muscles are mush. Don't wake me until noon. I feel as if I've paddled the entire length of the Colorado River in a canoe."

ELEVEN

John Mahoney, Chief of Security at the Zodiac, opened the door to the surveillance room and went in. "You wanted to see me, Bob?" he asked the man who sat at a console across from a wall banked with video screens. Every screen was filled with pictures relayed from the cameras downstairs in the casino.

"Yeah, Chief. Cliff, one of the night men, asked me to take a look at some film from last night. On a couple of roulette tables."

"Something wrong?"

Bob frowned. "I'm not sure. Maybe not. Probably not. On the surface, everything seems to look okay, but something in my gut . . ."

He didn't have to finish the thought. John had been working security in Vegas for twenty years. Sometimes instinct was more reliable than videotapes. And Bob was a good man.

"Let's have a look." John sat in one of the other two chairs at the console and waited for Bob to slip in the first tape. What he saw was a pretty, dark-haired woman winning fairly consistently. And getting damned excited about it. She'd raked in a good amount, then left in a rush. A blond man who stood nearby, but didn't play, cashed her in. When Bob stopped the tape, he said, "So?"

"Like I said, nothing on the surface. But take a look at this one." Bob slid another film in and hit a button to play it.

The same woman playing at a different table. The same man standing near the wheel but not playing. With one or two exceptions, she hit the numbers every time. And won big, big enough to draw a crowd.

"What's the problem?" John said. "I don't see how they could be cheating."

"I don't know exactly. Just something nagging in my gut."

"The woman looks familiar, but I can't put my finger on where I've seen her. I'll talk to the pit bosses and floor men on duty last night, see if they noticed anything unusual. Maybe she's just having a run of luck. It'll play out. It always does." He stood. "Save the tapes, just in case."

Mahoney went back to his office and drew himself another cup of coffee from the urn. He sat down at his desk and picked up the morning paper to glance at before he started on the mound of paperwork that always seemed to grow a foot overnight.

A picture on the front page caught his eye, and he tapped the woman's face with his finger. "That's where I've seen her." The woman on Bob's tape was Amy Jordan, the one who'd pulled that kid out of the water at the Valhalla.

He picked up his phone and punched out an extension.

TWELVE

After several days in Las Vegas, Amy and Neil had settled into a sort of routine. They ate when they were hungry, went sight-seeing when the mood struck them, gambled at different casinos two or three hours each day, and often practiced with dice and slots for an hour or two—though his greatest proficiency was still roulette. They usually chose one show an evening from among the many offerings of the various hotels. The rest of their time was spent sleeping or making love, more often than not, they chose the latter.

They couldn't seem to get enough of each other. In fact, they discovered that while Neil's psychokinetic abilities seemed to wane when he'd been at it too long, using them had another rather interesting side effect. He became more virile.

Amy was delighted. He was a marvelous lover. In fact she was getting quite addicted to the man in every way. Not only was he gorgeous, considerate, and great fun to be around, but they could actually hold stimulating conversations. He even sensed when she needed some space and hied himself off to the gym or some solitary activity so she could spend a couple of hours by herself.

That morning she'd spent her time in an intimate, but one-sided, relationship with a Megabucks slot machine in the Zodiac's casino. She had given, it had taken.

She'd just finished washing her hands and was about to meet Neil for lunch—they were planning to try a place that advertised great soul food—when she spotted Melissa Rowen huddled on a couch in the ladies' room, sobbing.

Amy's heart constricted. She sat down beside the young woman and rubbed her back. The cotton of her blouse was whisper thin from numerous washings. "Melissa? Remember me? Amy Jordan. We met the other night. What's wrong?"

The young woman looked up, a lost, desperate expression on her face. "Carl's upstairs, and he's locked himself in the room. I don't know what to do. He won't come out, and he won't let me in. I'm afraid he's going to do something awful."

"Like what?" Amy asked, afraid of the answer.

"I don't know. Something awful. His luck turned bad. He lost all that money. Everything. Not only didn't we get the money for Stacy's operation, but he used up all his paycheck and now we can't even pay our rent back home or buy groceries." She wailed, and tears poured down her cheeks.

"Oh, Melissa, I'm sorry." She gathered the distraught woman in her arms and stroked her back. "Listen now, I want you to stop crying. I have an idea."

The sobs slowed. "You do?"

"Yes. I have oodles of money. I'll give you enough for Stacy's operation with a little left over."

Melissa drew back and searched Amy's face with tear-reddened eyes. "You'd do that for a perfect stranger?"

"Of course I would. Come with me to the cashier's desk, and I'll get a check for you right now on one condition. You take it, go upstairs and get Carl, and go straight home. A deal?"

Melissa's face brightened, then slowly dimmed. "I don't think Carl would let me take it. It's kind of like taking charity, and he's real proud."

Amy rolled her eyes heavenward and thought, *And real dumb too.* Only an idiot would risk money he couldn't afford at a place like Las Vegas. She searched her brain trying to find a way to help this young family out of the mess they'd gotten themselves into.

An idea hit her.

She smiled.

"Melissa, how would Carl feel about taking money you won?"

"Okay, I guess, but I don't know how to gamble. And even if I did, I don't have any money, except for my lucky two-dollar bill. I keep it tucked away under my driver's license so I won't spend it."

"A two-dollar bill? Boy, I'd like to have one of those. I'll give you a hundred dollars for it."

The blonde's eyes widened. "A *hundred* dollars for a two-dollar bill?"

"Yep. Will you trade?"

"Well . . . sure, but that's crazy. Why would you want to do a thing like that?"

Amy shrugged. "I'm eccentric. And you need a stake to play roulette."

"But I don't know how to play roulette."

"That's okay. I'll teach you. Now you wash your face, and let's go find Neil."

"Who's Neil?"

Amy smiled. "My special fella."

With one arm hooked through Melissa's and the other through Neil's, she marched purposefully toward the roulette table.

"I thought we were going to have lunch," Neil said in an undertone. "You want to explain to me what this is all about?"

"I'll tell you later," she whispered out of the side of her mouth. In a normal voice, she said, "I'm going to teach Melissa to play roulette using our special method." Amy gave him an exaggerated wink, then another for good measure. "Won't that be fun?" She poked him in the ribs.

"Sure." He smiled. "Melissa, are you enjoying Las Vegas?"

Melissa, whose expression had resembled a dazed rabbit's ever since Amy had spirited her from the ladies' room, said timidly, "Not very much."

"Her husband had a run of bad luck, but I have a feeling that Melissa's luck is going to be very good. Isn't that right, Melissa?"

"If you say so."

"I do. This looks like a good table. What do

you think, Neil? Does this look like a lucky table to you?"

He shrugged. "Looks good to me."

Amy reached up to kiss his cheek and whispered softly. "Make sure that she wins big. *Please*."

An indulgent smile flashed over his lips. He nodded.

Neil took up his place near the wheel. Amy handed the dealer a hundred to buy in and had to pry the crumpled hundred she'd traded Melissa from her clutched fist to buy five-dollar chips for her.

"I'm going to teach my friend here to play roulette," Amy told the dealer. "She's a little nervous."

"I can see that," the dealer said, smiling as she pushed a stack of blue chips toward Amy and yellow ones toward Melissa.

Amy gave Melissa a quick rundown on inside bets, outside bets, and odds, but she could tell that everything she said went right over Melissa's head. "You'll get the hang of it as we go along. For now, just put a couple of chips on any three numbers you want."

"But I can't decide."

Amy sighed. This wasn't going to be easy. "Tell you what—everywhere I put my blue ones, you put your yellow ones, okay? Can you do that?"

She nodded.

Amy put two chips on six, two on eighteen, two on twenty-one. Melissa reluctantly followed suit.

The wheel turned; the ball spun.

"No more bets, please."

Clack.

Six.

Amy squealed and hugged her young friend.

"What happened?" Melissa asked.

"We won!"

"We did?"

"Yep. Let's try it again."

With a lot of coaching from Amy and a little razzle-dazzle with judiciously placed outside bets in addition to bets placed on inside numbers, their stack of chips grew to huge piles. A small crowd had gathered to watch them play and cheer them on. Amy tried to ignore the onlookers, but Melissa grew more and more nervous.

When Amy calculated that Melissa had close to thirty-five thousand dollars, she said, "Whew! I'm tired. Let's stop and have a drink. Cash us in," she said to the dealer.

The dealer counted their chips and returned trays of large denomination chips to each of them. After leaving a hefty tip on the table, Amy shepherded away Melissa, who looked even more dazed than when they'd begun.

After the three of them sat down at a table in the bar and ordered soft drinks, Melissa looked up from the tray she clutched to her chest and said, "Did I win a lot?"

"You won a lot. Neil, would you mind counting Melissa's winnings?" She peeled Melissa's fingers away from the chip holder and handed it to him.

Grinning, he dutifully totaled her chips while the women sipped their drinks.

"Well," he said after a few moments, "it looks like thirty-six thousand, two hundred."

Melissa sputtered into her drink and began coughing. She patted her chest until the fit stopped, then looked at Amy with eyes grown unbelievably wide. "Did he say thirty-six *thousand*?"

"And two hundred."

"Dollars?"

"Yep." Amy grinned. "Looks like this was your lucky day."

"It was you who did it. I don't know exactly how, and I'm not asking. But thank you, thank you, thank you." Laughing, Melissa threw her arms around Amy and hugged her. "Wait until I tell Carl. He's gonna die. He's just gonna *die*!"

"Before you do that," Amy said, "I have an idea about what you should do with the money. Which bank do you use back home?"

Luckily, the Rowens' bank was one that had a branch in the hotel. Neil and Amy went with her to deposit most of Melissa's windfall in a savings account to cover Stacy's surgery and with extra for emergencies. Melissa kept out a few hundred—to have some fun with, Amy had told her—and tucked it into her cracked plastic purse.

Outside the bank, Melissa hugged both of them again. "I can't tell you how much I appreciate this. I don't know how I can ever make it up to you. Except maybe—" She blushed and glanced down. "Well, I haven't told Carl about it yet, 'cause I didn't want to heap any extra worries on him right now, but I'm gonna have another baby."

Amy squeezed her hand. "Oh, Melissa, that's wonderful."

"I thought maybe . . . well, if you wouldn't mind . . . I thought maybe I could name it Amy if it's a girl or Neil if it's a boy." She glanced up shyly. "Would that be all right?"

Amy beamed. "That would be wonderful! Wouldn't it, Neil?" She glanced at him and noticed that his smile was especially bright too.

"Yes, it would," he said. "And quite an honor."

They said their good-byes. Amy and Neil stood, arms around each other's waists, and watched Melissa walk away, as if floating on air.

Amy leaned her head against Neil's shoulder and sighed. "Her husband got carried away and lost all their money. Now their little girl can have surgery, they can pay their bills, and they'll have some for the new baby too. Doesn't that make you feel simply glorious?"

He nuzzled her forehead. "You really enjoy doing that sort of thing, don't you?"

She nodded. "That's what the world is all about. Helping people. Making life better, richer, and happier for everyone."

"Including me?"

She smiled. "Especially you."

"Good. Let's go deposit this tray of chips and attend to my appetite. I'm starved."

Knowing how using his psychokinetic power affected his sex drive, she giggled. "For what?"

He chuckled. "For that too. But let's eat first, and we can spend the rest of the afternoon doing . . . other things."

❖━━━━━━━━❖

Chief of Security John Mahoney and Ken Underwood, an investigator with gambling control, sat in the Zodiac's surveillance room reviewing the latest tape for the third time.

"Bringing this other woman in is a new twist," Underwood said, "but for the life of me, I can't see what they're doing to cheat. We've had a man on them since you called. Even though they play here more often, they've won big at several of the hotels. And their MO is the same every time. She plays roulette, and he watches. They never play for more than two or three hours. Switching dealers doesn't change her luck, the pit bosses haven't picked up on anything, and we've checked the wheels they've played for every possible device. Nothing. But—"

"But?"

"Oh hell, John, you and I have been around long enough to see some strange things. It might just be a crazy run of luck. It happens."

"But you don't think this is just luck?"

"I don't know." Underwood frowned and chewed on the inside of his cheek. "I've got a funny feeling about this one. Maybe we should put a man on the blond woman too."

Mahoney shook his head. "She's checked out. Left to go back to Farmington, New Mexico, an hour ago. She and her husband were just a couple of kids who won a trip to Vegas in a drawing from a local radio station. I don't see how they can be hooked up to this thing."

Underwood gave a snort. "What thing?"

"Now that's the question, isn't it?"

"That's the question. We'll keep a man on them. If something squirrelly's going on, we'll figure it out. But I can tell you right now, I've got a hunch that this is one for the books."

"We've got one good thing going for us," Mahoney said.

"What's that?"

"She has lousy luck at the slots."

Amy lay curled against Neil, her head tucked in the crook of his shoulder, her finger toying with one of the tiny scars on his chest.

"Happy?" he asked.

"Very." She kissed the small scar, then stretched, still feeling deliciously mellow from making love. "We've made a lot of money for your laboratory. How much more do you think we need?"

He was quiet for a moment. "Oh, I don't know. Lots. Anything special you want to do today? How about the Liberace Museum? I've been reading about it, and it sounds sort of interesting."

She laughed. "The *Liberace* Museum?"

"Or we could go shopping. How about that? I saw you drooling over some of those dresses in that shop at Caesars. Let's go buy a couple for you."

"Neil, those were *designer* dresses. They cost the earth."

He chuckled. "It's not as if we don't have plenty of money."

"But that's your lab money, it's not money money. I'd feel guilty squandering it."

He heaved a deep sigh. After a moment he said, "Tell you what. I'm going to give the crap table a try today, strictly as an experiment. Let's consider anything I win ours to play around with. Okay?"

After considering the matter, she agreed. "I want to wash my hair. I'll meet you downstairs at the Megabucks slots in two hours."

"Washing your hair takes two hours?"

She grinned. "No. I thought I'd spend a little time on the slots."

He laughed. "You and those slots. I don't know what your fascination is with them. You always lose." He growled and playfully gnawed at her throat. "Stick with me, kid, and I'll make you rich."

❖―――――❖

Amy was down to her last four dollars from the second roll she'd opened. She put in three and pushed the button.

One cherry. Two dollars. Big deal. Enough for one more play.

She wasn't having much luck at the machines. Maybe other people knew something that she didn't because the row of stools at the Megabucks slots was practically deserted. Nobody was playing except a wizened little grayhaired man four machines down and her. She hadn't heard much action from his machine either, but he had several rows of silver dollars in a tray and a white glove on his right hand. A serious player. Maybe she ought to get a glove to keep her hand clean and her fingernails from chipping.

A guy who appeared to be in his midtwenties, slick looking and thin in a slightly emaciated way, sat down on the stool next to the old man and began to play slowly, putting in only one dollar at a time.

That struck her as peculiar. She watched him from the corner of her eye as she fed her last three coins to the slot.

One cherry again. Two dollars.

She sat there for a moment, contemplating what to do. If she put in only two dollars and hit, she could miss the big jackpot. Should she open another roll of change, or should she call it quits and wait for Neil? He would be along anytime now.

Deciding that she would quit, she scooped her two dollars from the trough and grabbed the strap of her shoulder bag. Something made her glance to her left, and just in time she saw the young man toss a dollar on the floor and say something to the old man.

When the old man bent to pick up the dollar, the young man grabbed the old gent's tray of coins and made a break with them. As the skinny guy dashed by her, Amy whipped out her shoulder bag by the strap. It tangled around his legs like a bola, and he fell flat on his face. Coins went everywhere.

"Thief! Thief!" the old man yelled.

The young guy scuttled like a crab trying to get away, but two men were on him in a shot, one a uniformed casino guard, the other a man in a suit. As the man in the suit wrestled the struggling thief to the floor, Amy saw the flash of a holstered gun beneath his jacket and figured that he was a plainclothes casino man.

Boy, the security in the place was impressive.

Neil's heart was in his throat. He'd watched the whole thing from not more than twenty feet away. He hadn't realized at first what was happening. He'd thought that Amy had accidentally tripped someone with her purse, but when he realized that she was in the middle of a robbery, he'd almost gone berserk getting to her.

He grabbed her and crushed her to him. "Are you all right?"

"I'm fine," she said a little breathlessly, "except that you're squeezing the life out of me."

He relaxed his hold and searched her face, expecting to find her distressed and in need of reassurance.

She was grinning. "Ho-ly mo-ley, did you see that? I dropped that sucker dead in his tracks."

She was actually enjoying the whole thing. He didn't know whether to shake her or laugh. He laughed. And hugged her again. "Whatever possessed you to do something like that?"

She shrugged. "Reflex action I guess. But I do hate it when people try to rip off old folks. It makes my blood boil!"

"Remind me never to get you riled. Especially when you're packing your purse."

The old man hurried up to them, making excited gestures. He grabbed Amy's hand and kissed it. "I am Sol Goldman," he said. "You saved my money from that thief. I am most grateful."

"You're most welcome, Mr. Goldman. Did you recover everything?"

"I think so. The guards are gathering it up."

One of the guards approached and politely asked that they all come with him to the security office so that a report could be filed. They saw the thief being taken away in handcuffs as they accompanied the guard and Mr. Goldman to the elevators.

Upstairs, John Mahoney introduced himself and greeted them cordially, apologizing for the incident that had required their presence. After his secretary had taken everyone's statements, he kept Amy and Neil in his office after the others had gone.

Mahoney, a middle-aged man who Neil thought looked like a Marine in civilian clothes, said to Amy, "The hotel would like to do something to show its appreciation, but I understand that you're already a heroine and receiving the VIP treatment. Maybe we ought to hire you." He laughed jovially. "Or give you the key to the city. Are you enjoying yourselves in our town?"

They both assured him that they were, and he continued to chat with them for several minutes before ushering them from his office with an admonition to call him personally if they needed anything.

Only as they went downstairs in the elevator did Neil realize how slickly Mahoney had extracted their entire backgrounds in a few minutes.

As they came off the elevator, Amy stopped. "With all the hullabaloo I haven't had a chance to ask you how you did at the crap table."

Neil grinned, reached in his pocket, and pulled out the thick wad of bills. When Amy's eyes widened and she uttered her usual, "Ho-ly mo-ley," he threw back his head and laughed.

"Neil," she said, glancing around, "put that back in your pocket. You shouldn't be carrying so much cash. If that guy was so bold as to steal Mr. Goldman's dollars, there are bound to be lowlifes around who would bash you over the head in a flash for that much money."

Chuckling, he stuck the money in his pocket and hugged her against him. "I figure I'm safe as long as you have your purse. What all do you have in that thing anyhow?"

"Just the usual essentials." She grinned. "And four rolls of silver dollars."

"Come on," Neil said, "let's go shopping."

They bought ice-cream cones at one of the shops and ate them as they strolled the few blocks to Caesars Palace. Along the way they stopped to watch the volcano blow in front of The Mirage. They were finished with the cones by the time they arrived at the front entrance of Caesars.

Inside, Amy spotted a group of people waiting to ride Cleopatra's Barge, the opulent gold boat that traveled on a man-made waterway inside the hotel.

"Oh, let's ride it," she said to Neil. "It looks like fun." She checked her watch and glanced at the schedule. "Boarding is in about five minutes."

"Fine with me."

They joined the group waiting.

She had just turned to say something to Neil when he said, "Hey!"

She saw him struggling with two men, one of whom had his hand in Neil's pocket. While he wrestled with one, she yelled and swung her purse at the other.

He threw up his arms to defend himself, but she got in a couple of good whacks and had him on his knees before what he was shouting soaked in.

"Lady, stop! I'm one of the good guys. I'm with gambling control."

She stopped, and he pulled an ID from his suit pocket. She looked at the ID, then back at him, then at Neil who had her hugged to his side like a Siamese twin.

"Looks authentic," Neil said. "What were you doing?"

"Trying to stop the guy who had his hand in your pocket. He got away. Did he get your money?"

Neil felt in his jacket. "No, it's still there. Sorry about the mix-up. Thanks."

"It's not wise to carry a large amount of cash around. You're inviting trouble if you do. I'd suggest that you put it someplace safe," the man said.

"That's exactly what I told him," Amy piped up.

"Let's go spend it right now," Neil said.

"But I thought we were going to ride—" She glanced over her shoulder. The crowd was gone except for a few stragglers who were openly gawking at them.

"Honey, I'm afraid we missed the boat."

"Oh, rats!"

He laughed. "Come on. Let's go shopping. I still want to buy you those dresses, and I need to get rid of this cash."

As they walked through the casino toward one of the pricey boutiques, Amy said, "You know, something about that guy from gambling control looked familiar. I could swear that I've seen him before."

"Maybe he has one of those faces."

"Maybe so. What is gambling control anyhow?"

Neil shrugged. "Some sort of security, I suppose."

"There may be a lot of thieves in this town, but I'll say one thing for them, their security is on the ball. Why, that guy no sooner had his hand in your pocket than, *bam*, that gambling control guy was right there. Impressive."

THIRTEEN

John Mahoney, Ken Underwood, and two other gambling control investigators sat in the surveillance room of the Zodiac. They had looked at the latest tape a half dozen times.

"I'll tell you one thing," Underwood said. "He's either the slickest crook or the luckiest son of a bitch I've ever run across."

"And a hell of a craps player," one of the other agents interjected. "Cooler than an igloo in Alaska."

Mahoney shook his head. "If he or the woman are cheating, I can't figure out how they're doing it. And they're nice people too. Hell, she's a blooming heroine twice over. She's a social worker, and he's a Ph.D. Does some kind of work in cancer research."

One agent touched his head gingerly. "She

packs a devil of a wallop for a social worker. She must keep rocks in that purse of hers."

The other agents laughed.

Mahoney swiped a beefy hand across his face. "What do you think we ought to do?"

Underwood shrugged. "I can't find any reason to justify keeping men on them. We've stuck to them like sweet on sugar and come up empty."

"I think you're right," Mahoney said. "All we can hope is that Lady Luck turns her back on them or they leave town soon. I can't figure—" He hesitated, rubbed his chin, and frowned.

"Think of something?" an agent asked.

"I was just remembering a crazy phone call I had a couple of weeks ago. But, naw, it's nothing. How about we put out the cat and close the door on this one? Let's go have a cup of coffee."

FOURTEEN

In the living room of their suite, lit only by the flickering of the gas logs in the fireplace and the night sky beyond the open draperies, Amy lay naked on one of the couches. Neil knelt beside her dribbling Dom Pérignon into her navel and sipping from it.

She giggled, and he quickly licked a drop that sloshed over and ran down. "Neil Larkin, I swear you're becoming more decadent by the day."

He chuckled against her belly. "That's not decadent, love. I'll show you decadent." He reached for the champagne bottle and lifted her hips.

"Neil! You wouldn't!"

A slow grin spread over his face. "The hell I wouldn't."

He did.

"Ho-ly mo-ley," she moaned.

He did it again.

"What are you doing to me?" she gasped, writhing under the touch of his tongue.

"Loving you."

With champagne, hot breath, and wet tongue he sent her sailing out over the moon. To Venus. Beyond.

She cried out as an unbelievable climax seized her. Its fluttering ripples went on and on and on.

When she lay sated and mellow, he rubbed his cheek over her damp belly. "Have I ever told you how much I love to touch you? How much I love to watch you? How much I love you?"

She stiffened. "What did you say?"

"I said that I love you. Is that a surprise?"

"Yes. No. I don't know. I—I hadn't thought about it."

Liar, she told herself. She'd thought about it. Often. But she hadn't wanted to admit that love might be creeping into their relationship. Hadn't she promised herself that she wouldn't get too involved? Their divergent lives had intersected briefly, and once they left Las Vegas, who knew where his would lead him and hers would take her to?

"Think about it," he said, kissing her hip. "In the meantime, I have a surprise for you."

He stood and, completely comfortable with his beautiful nakedness, walked over to where he'd dropped his new silk jacket. And he was beautiful. More beautiful than any of the sculpted gods lining Caesars drive. Much more beautiful than she whose hips were a tad too wide and whose face was much too ordinary. Strange that he never seemed to notice her flaws. Maybe he needed a vision correction.

He returned with a long velvet box and opened it.

"What is it?"

"Lie down and close your eyes. I want to put it on first."

She did as he asked, and she felt him place something around her ankle. "What is it?" She opened her eyes and held up her foot.

Firelight caught the shimmering sparkle of diamonds circling her ankle. "Like it?"

"It's magnificent, but, Neil, what have you done?"

He smiled. "Bought you a pretty bauble. From my winnings at the Golden Nugget crap table." He knelt beside her once more, stroked her outer thigh and rested his chin on her hipbone.

She sighed. "You can't keep buying me expensive gifts."

"Why not? I can afford it, and I like to buy you pretty things."

A gradual change in his behavior over the past several days that had been only a niggling concern before, blossomed into a full-fledged alarm bell. "Neil, there's something we need to discuss."

"And what is that?" He circled one breast with his tongue.

"Stop that! I can't think when you're touching me."

He drew back and sat on the floor with his arms around his knees. "Sounds serious."

"It is." She sat up and pulled a pillow in front of her to shield her nudity. It was difficult to have a philosophical discussion completely naked. "It seems to me that we're getting off the track, losing sight of why we're here. The whole idea of coming to Las Vegas was not to run and play but to make enough money for you to open a research laboratory. I don't feel that you're still focused on that goal. Am I wrong?"

His silence stretched endlessly.

Finally he said, "I've been meaning to talk to you about that."

More silence.

Her alarm grew.

"Since I was kicked out of the biomedical conference in New Orleans, I've done a lot of thinking. Amy, I'm not sure that I'm cut out to be a scientist."

"But, Neil, that's ridiculous. You—"

He held up a hand. "Let me explain. I've told you about Gran and why I got into the field of cancer research. It was anger that drove me, not any true burning passion for the profession. Even so, for the past several years, I've focused every ounce of my energy and attention on my research, lived and breathed the lab and my work. It took getting booted out and meeting you for me to discover that I didn't enjoy what I was doing. I found more satisfaction in baking bread than I ever found in studying slides. I don't want a laboratory. I don't want to go back into research."

Stunned by his admission, she couldn't speak for a moment. She could barely breathe. The pedestal she'd placed him on was crumbling fast. "Then what do you want to do?" she asked softly.

"I suppose what I've discovered I do best." He smiled. "Make money. Live the good life. Give you the world. You want to travel? We can go anywhere you'd like. We can climb the Pyramids in Egypt, throw coins in the fountain in

Rome, take a gondola through the canals in Venice, stop off to replenish our coffers in Monte Carlo or the Caribbean—"

Horrified by his words, she interrupted shrilly, "You want us to become hedonistic *lumps*?"

He laughed. "Oh, but what a lovely lump you'll be. I'll smother you in diamonds and rubies and sapphires, buy you a Ferrari and a villa in the south of France. Anything you want." He tried to gather her into his arms, but she struggled against him. "Sweetheart, what's wrong?"

Shoving him away, she jumped to her feet. "What's wrong?" she shrieked. "What's *wrong*? Oh God, get away from me. I don't know you." Tears began to flow.

"Amy, love—" He reached for her, but she slapped his hands away. "What's gotten into you?"

"Into *me*? How could you, Neil? How could you?" She was yelling like a fishwife, but she didn't care. She was unraveling inside. "How could you betray all the people who are suffering and dying when you could do something about it? When you're this close, this close"— she measured a fraction of an inch with her fingers—"to finding a cure for cancer. For *cancer*, dammit!" She clamped her hands over her head. "Oh God, I can't believe this."

"Amy, let me explain—"

"I've heard your explanations! I don't want to hear any more about diamonds and Venice and Monte Carlo. I don't give a damn about those things! I care about people. I—" A sob broke off her words, and she fled to a bedroom and slammed the door.

Neil banged on the door. "Dammit, Amy, listen to me. You don't understand. Open the door. Talk to me." He hammered and hammered with his fist. He shouted until he was hoarse. Nothing.

Feeling as if his soul had been ripped out, he leaned his forehead against the thick door. She didn't understand. She hadn't figured out that he could never go back into research. Or why.

He knew. He had wrestled with the knowledge for days now.

His colleagues had been right.

His experiments had been totally useless.

As he walked away, an agony of spirit tore at his chest, brought him to his knees. Losing Amy would be the greatest blow of all. He had to make her understand.

He did the only thing he could think to do. He drank champagne until he found oblivion.

Amy rose before dawn, giving up sleep as a lost cause. She'd only dozed sporadically between bouts of weeping and cursing. She had shared Neil's dream, admired his altruistic spirit, believed in him and his work. She'd seen him as an idol of all that was right and pure in human nature.

But now, now she felt betrayed to the depths of her inner most being. Seduced by visions of wealth and selfish pleasure in a neon city with no substance, he'd sold out. Flushed his offering to the world down the toilet.

He was as shallow as Michael. No, he was worse than her ex-fiancé. Michael had never had high principles to begin with.

How could she have been so blind? How could she believe that she might have loved him?

Did love him.

Oh, God.

Maybe there was some way she could reason with him, make him see what he would be throwing away to turn his back on his scientific work. Maybe she could make him understand that sometimes personal sacrifice was a small price to pay for something that would be of such tremendous benefit to the world.

Yes, she had to try. For her sake. For his.

She rose, wrapped herself in one of the terry hotel robes, and went to the door.

Cautiously, she stuck her head out. A chilled quiet met her. She searched the bedroom they shared first. It was empty. Padding on bare feet to the living room, she found Neil sprawled naked on a couch, snoring, an empty champagne bottle beside him.

The whole scene struck her as reminiscent of the aftermath of an orgy, a pagan bacchanal. Fury rose up anew. How dare he drink himself into a sybaritic stupor while she was suffering!

Damn his gorgeous eyes and miserable hide!

She stomped back to their bedroom, called the airport, and packed her bag.

Amy had been sitting in the restaurant for two and a half hours waiting for the first seat out on a plane to New Orleans. She hated to fall in on Rachel, but she had nowhere else to go.

She sipped her third cup of coffee, now grown cold, and wallowed in her misery.

She'd had time to do some thinking in the unforgiving light of day, time to examine her own motives, and she didn't like what she saw. She'd been unfair to Neil. She'd sculpted his image according to her vision and put him up on that high pedestal herself. Something one of her college professors once said came to mind: It's damned hard to pee when you're on a pedestal.

Neil wasn't a god; he was a human being.

The whole notion of developing his psychokinetic ability, coming to Las Vegas, funding a new research laboratory, and saving the world through his efforts had been her idea, not his. Little Miss Do-Gooder rushing in to rescue a lost soul, whether he wanted rescuing or not. Pushing him around. Managing his life. Fixing everything. Her usual modus operandi.

Well, this time she'd screwed up good.

Now that she looked back over the time since she'd first met Neil, it didn't help to realize that everything he'd done had been to please her. All she'd done was mess up his head and mess up his life.

She checked her watch and sighed. Her plane would be boarding in a few minutes. She might as well wander on down to the gate. Still she'd hoped . . .

No, he was well rid of her.

Amy rose, hoisted her purse over her shoulder, and paid her check.

As she walked down the concourse, she heard the ding and clink of slot machines in the boarding area. The last time she'd been here, her mood had been very different, full of excitement and hope.

She looked at the change in her hand from the restaurant. Three quarters.

She shrugged. Why not? Finding a machine with cherries, she fed the three coins into the slot, took a deep breath, and pushed the spin button.

One cherry.

Two cherries.

Three cherries.

Four.

Bells rang, lights flashed, and quarters spewed out. They kept coming and coming, clinking fast and furiously, filling up the metal bin.

Something made her glance over her left shoulder. Less than five feet away, leaning against a post and with his hands in his pockets, stood Neil. His hair was rumpled, he needed a shave, but he was grinning.

"I see you finally hit one," he said.

"Yes, I did," she said smugly. Then her eyes narrowed. "Did you—?"

He laughed.

"You did!"

He stepped closer. "Does it matter?"

"No, not really."

He lifted her chin and scanned her face with those beautiful blue, blue eyes. "Amy, I love you."

Tears clogged her throat and stung her eyes.

"Please don't leave. At least until we've had a chance to talk. Would you do that for me?"

She nodded. "But my bags, the plane."

"I'll handle it." He headed toward the check-in desk to speak with an attendant.

Amy started to follow when a man said, "Lady, don't forget your money."

She looked down at the pile of quarters and laughed. It took two buckets to hold them all.

With her bags stowed in the trunk of the red Cadillac convertible, Neil drove back to the Zodiac. He'd asked her to return to their suite so that they could talk in private. She'd agreed.

When they arrived, the rooms had been cleaned. Beds were made, the champagne bottle gone. He seemed very nervous as he led her to the couch and sat in a chair across from her.

He took her hands in his. "Amy, you left last night before you heard the entire story. I explained things badly. I know how much you believed in me and in the work I was doing. God, so did I. You can't imagine how exciting, how gratifying it is to think that you've discovered a drug that can cure one of the world's most dreaded diseases. When I thought I had it, every hour I had worked, every sleepless night I'd spent, every sacrifice I'd made was worth it. I'd go through it all again if I knew I could save Gran's life . . . or anyone's life.

"But, Amy, I can't. I understand now why no one could replicate my research. The substance never worked."

"But you wouldn't have cheated!"

"No, not consciously. But in a way I did."

She frowned. "I don't understand."

"I wanted that drug to work so badly that I must have influenced it unconsciously. Psychokinetically."

A terrible sinking feeling flooded her. She squeezed his hands. "Oh, Neil, no."

He shrugged casually, but she saw the pain in his eyes. "So you see, sweetheart, even if I wanted to go back into biomedical research, it's no place for me. I could never trust my findings."

"Neil, I'm sorry. I'm so sorry for being an insensitive idiot. I should have listened to you last night instead of getting on my self-righteous high horse." She sniffed.

He moved beside her on the couch and pulled her into his arms. "Shhh. Don't cry about it. All that fervent compassion is one of the things I love about you. Your heart is bigger than the Megabucks jackpot. And I didn't mean to sound like such a hedonistic lump. I was just trying to think up ways to make you happy. All I want is for us to be together and for you to be happy. I love you."

"I love you too," she sobbed, burying her face against his shoulder.

He laughed and hugged her tight. "I'm glad to hear it. You had me sweating there for a while. As long as you love me, we can work the other stuff out. We can open our own bakery somewhere if that's what you want to do."

"A *bakery*? And get up at three o'clock in the morning? God forbid. But I have an idea—"

He kissed her. "And I'd like to hear all about it. Later."

Amy lay contented as a cat in Neil's arms. The bottom of her foot absently slid up and down his shin while her finger toyed with one of the small scars on his chest. "Want to hear my idea now?"

He kissed her forehead. "Sure."

She scrambled up on her hands and knees to face him. "Well, I've been thinking. You do have this special gift, and I feel that we ought to make the most of it. Now I know research is out, but think of all the other things we can do to help—like with Melissa and Carl. We can quietly find people who need a leg up and play Santa Claus. There are other kids who need surgery; there are tons of people who need things that our money can provide. We could set up some sort of foundation maybe and do it all secretly so that no one would know where the money came from. Doesn't that sound like a grand idea?"

"You thought up all that while we were making love?" he asked, his tone amused.

"No, silly, it came to me in a flash before."

He pulled her against him and kissed her nose. "I think it does sound like a grand idea. We'll forget about diamonds and Rome and Venice."

She snuggled back against his chest. "Welllll, Venice might not be such a bad idea."

"It's supposed to be a great place for a honeymoon."

She stilled. "Are you trying to say something?"

"Uh-huh. Want to come home with me Thanksgiving and meet my family?"

She nodded. "I wish I could have met your grandmother."

"So do I. Gran would have loved you."

EPILOGUE

On New Year's Eve in a small wedding chapel in Las Vegas, Neil's parents, his five brothers and sisters and assorted spouses and offspring, joined with Amy's sister Rachel, their mother and stepfather, and two maiden aunts for the nuptials.

The room was filled with the sweet scent of dozens of red roses and the flickering warmth of white candles. Neil stood with his brother Tom beside the altar where a robed minister attended in readiness.

Neil's brother Link played the wedding march softly on his guitar. In a few moments, Rachel, dressed in wine velvet entered. Neil waited, breath held, eyes on the entryway for Amy.

He had never seen her more beautiful.

Her dress was long white satin, trimmed with lace and beaded with crystals and pearls that caught the light and turned her into an angel. Although a filmy veil covered her face, he could see the brightness of the smile that had stolen his heart from the first moment he saw her.

She drew near and stood beside him. They joined hands as Link sang a love song he'd written for the occasion and was sure to be his next hit single.

When the last strain died, the minister began the ceremony. Their voices were clear and filled with love as they repeated their vows.

"You may kiss the bride," the minister said.

Neil grinned, and Amy's veil rose as if by magic. She smiled as she heard the minister gasp.

John Mahoney punched a number on his phone. When Ken Underwood answered, he said, "They're back."

THE EDITOR'S CORNER

At this time of year there is always much to be thankful for, not the least of which are the four terrific romances coming your way next month. These stories are full of warmth, passion, and love—just the thing for those cold winter nights. So make a date to snuggle up under a comforter and read the LOVE-SWEPTs we have in store for you. They're sure to heat up your reading hours with their witty and sensuous tales.

The wonderfully talented Terry Lawrence starts things off with a hero who's **A MAN'S MAN**, LOVESWEPT #718. From the moment Reilly helps Melissa Drummond into the helicopter, she is enthralled—mesmerized by this man of mystery who makes her feel safe and threatened all at once! Sensing the needs she's long denied, he tempts her to taste desire, to risk believing in a love that will last. Once he's warned her that he'll woo her until he's won, she must trust his promises enough to vow her own. This tale of irresistible courtship is another Terry Lawrence treasure.

THE COP AND THE MOTHER-TO-BE, LOVESWEPT #719, is the newest heartwarming romance from Charlotte Hughes. Jake Flannery had shared Sammie Webster's grief at losing her husband, cared for her as her child grew inside her, and flirted with her when she knew no one could find a puffy pregnant lady sexy—but she doesn't dare wonder why this tough cop's touch thrills her. And Jake tries not to imagine making love to the feisty mom or playing daddy to her daughter. But somehow their cherished friendship has turned to dangerous desire, and Jake must pull out all the stops to get Sammie to confess she'll adore him forever. The ever popular Charlotte Hughes offers a chance to laugh and cry and fall in love all over again.

Get ready for Lynne Bryant's **DAREDEVIL,** LOVESWEPT #720. Casey Boone is Dare King's buddy, his best friend, the only girl he's ever loved—but now that he might never walk again, Dare King struggles not to let her see his panic . . . or the pain he still feels three years after she left him at the altar! Casey has never stopped loving her proud warrior but fears losing him as she'd lost her dad. Now she must find the courage to heal Dare—body and soul—at last. In this touching and sizzling novel, Lynne Bryant explores the power of love, tested but enduring.

Linda Cajio wants you to meet an **IRRESISTIBLE STRANGER,** LOVESWEPT #721. Leslie Kloslosky doesn't believe her friend's premonition that she'll meet the perfect man on her vacation in

England—right up to the instant a tall, dark stranger enters the cramped elevator and lights a fire in her blood! Fascinated by the willowy brunette whose eyes turn dark sapphire when he kisses her, Mike Smith isn't about to let her go . . . but will he be clever enough to elude a pair of thieves hot on their trail? Linda Cajio weaves a treasured romantic fantasy you won't forget.

Happy reading!

With warmest wishes,

Beth de Guzman

Beth de Guzman

Senior Editor

P.S. Don't miss the women's novels coming your way in December: **ADAM'S FALL**, from blockbuster author Sandra Brown, is a deliciously sensual story of a woman torn between her duty and her heart; **PURE SIN**, from nationally bestselling author Susan Johnson, is a sensuous tale of thrilling seduction set in nineteenth-century Montana; **ON WINGS OF MAGIC**, by the award-winning Kay Hooper, is a classic contemporary romance of a woman who must make a choice between protecting her heart and surrendering to love once more. We'll be giving you a sneak peek at these wonderful books in next month's LOVESWEPTs. And immediately following this page look for a preview of the terrific romances from Bantam that are *available now!*

Don't miss these incomparable books
by your favorite Bantam authors

On sale in October

WANTED

by Patricia Potter

SCANDAL IN

SILVER

by Sandra Chastain

THE WINDFLOWER

by Sharon and Tom Curtis

Winner of the *Romantic Times* 1992
Storyteller of the Year Award

PATRICIA POTTER

NATIONALLY BESTSELLING AUTHOR OF *RELENTLESS* AND *NOTORIOUS*

WANTED

Texas Ranger Morgan Davis hadn't grown up with much love, but he had been raised with respect for duty and the law. To him, Lorilee Braden was nothing but a con artist, yet her fire and beauty drew him despite his better judgment. Still, her brother was wanted for murder—and the face on the wanted poster looked far too much like Morgan's for comfort. The only way he could clear his own name was to bring Nicholas Braden to justice . . . before the spark Lori had lit became a raging blaze that consumed everything Morgan believed in . . .

Braden balked at moving again. "Where's my sister?"

"In back," Morgan said. He led his prisoner to the tree several yards behind the cabin. The woman immediately saw Nicholas Braden, her eyes resting on the handcuffs for a moment, then she glared at Morgan.

Braden stepped over to his sister, stooped down,

and awkwardly pulled the gag from her mouth. "Are you all right?"

Morgan leaned back lazily against a tree and watched every movement, every exchange of silent message between the sister and brother. He felt a stab of longing, a regret that he'd never shared that kind of caring or communication with another human being.

Braden tried to untie his sister, but the handcuffs hindered him. Morgan heard a muffled curse and saw the woman's face tense with pain.

"Move away," Morgan said to Braden. Braden hesitated.

"Dammit, I'm not going to keep repeating myself." Irritation and impatience laced Morgan's words.

Braden stood, took a few steps away.

"Farther," Morgan ordered. "Unless you want her to stay there all night."

Braden backed up several feet, and Morgan knelt beside Lorilee Braden. With the knife from his belt, he quickly cut the strips of cloth binding her. Unfamiliar guilt rushed through him as he saw blood on her wrists. He hadn't tied her that tightly, but apparently the cloth had cut into her skin when she'd struggled to free herself.

His gaze met hers, and he was chilled by the contempt there. He put out his hand to help her up, but she refused it, trying to gain footing by herself. Her muscles must have stiffened because she started to fall.

Instinctively reaching out to help her, Morgan dropped the knife, and he saw her go for it. His foot slammed down on it. Then her hand went for the gun in Braden's gunbelt, which Morgan had slung over his shoulder.

Morgan swore as he spun her around, his hand going around her neck to subdue her. Out of the corner of his eye, he saw Nicholas Braden move toward him. "Don't," Morgan said. "I might just make a mistake and hurt her."

All rage and determination, she was quivering against him, defying him with every ounce of her being.

"You do real well against women, don't you?" Braden taunted.

Morgan had always had a temper—he felt ready to explode now—but his voice was even and cold when he spoke. "You'd better tell your sister to behave herself if she wants you to live beyond this day." His arms tightened around her. She wriggled to escape his hold, and he felt his body's reaction to it. It puzzled him. It infuriated him. He didn't like what he didn't understand, and he couldn't understand his reaction to this she-cat. She was trouble, pure trouble, but a part of him admired her, and he despised that admiration as a weakness in himself. "Tell her!"

"Lori."

Braden's voice was low but authoritative, and Morgan felt the girl relax slightly, then jerk away from him and run to her brother. Braden's handcuffed hands went over her head and around her, and he held her as she leaned trustingly against him. A criminal. A killer. A rare wave of loneliness swept over Morgan, flooding him with intense jealousy, nearly turning him inside out.

"Touching scene," he observed sarcastically, his voice rough as he tried to reestablish control—over his prisoner and the woman and over himself.

He tried to discipline his own body, to dismiss the

lingering flowery scent of Lorilee Braden, the remembered softness of her body against his. She was a hellion, he warned himself, not soft at all, except in body. He'd already underestimated her twice. He wouldn't do it again.

Scandal in Silver

By

Sandra Chastain

"This delightful author has a tremendous talent that places her on a pinnacle reserved for special romance writers."—*Affaire de Coeur*

Sandra Chastain is a true reader favorite, and with SCANDAL IN SILVER, her new "Once Upon a Time Romance," she borrows from Seven Brides for Seven Brothers *for a wonderfully funny and sensual historical romance about five sisters stranded in the Colorado wilderness with a silver mine.*

"What was that?" he said, and came to a full stop.

To her credit she didn't jump up or cry out. Instead she looked around slowly, tilting her head to listen to the sounds of the night.

"I don't hear anything, Colter."

"We're being watched. Stand up slowly. Hold out your hand and smile."

She followed his directions, but the smiling was hard. She was certain there was nothing out there and that he knew it. This was a ruse. She'd known not to trust him; this proved it. "Now what?"

He returned her smile, dropped his wood and started toward her, speaking under his breath. "When I take your hand I'm going to put my arms around you and we'll walk deeper into the trees."

"Why?"

"I don't know what's going to happen, and I don't want to be out in the open." He hoped she didn't stop to examine that bit of inane logic.

"Shall I bring the rifle?"

"No, that would give us away."

He clasped her hand and pulled her close, sliding his arm around her as he turned her away from the fire. After an awkward moment she fitted herself against him and matched her steps to his.

"Is this good?" she asked, throwing her head back and widening her smile recklessly. The motion allowed her hat to fall behind her, freeing her hair and exposing her face to the light. She was rewarded by the astonished expression on his face. Two could play games, she decided.

His smile vanished. "Yes!" he said hoarsely. "You're getting the idea. In fact—"

"Don't you dare say I'm beautiful again, Captain Colter. Even a fool would know you are only trying to frighten me." She was looking up at him, her eyes stormy, her mouth soft and inviting. "Why?"

"I'm not trying to frighten you," he answered. She couldn't know how appealing she was, or that she was tempting him to kiss her. And he couldn't resist the temptation. He curled his arm, bringing her around in front of him as he lowered his head. His lips touched hers. She froze.

"Easy," he whispered, brushing his lips back and forth against a mouth now clamped shut. She gasped, parting her lips, and he thrust his tongue inside. Her jacket fell open as he pressed against her, almost dizzy from the feel of her. He felt her arm creep around him. For a long, senseless moment he forgot what he'd started out to do. The kiss that was meant to distract Sabrina had an unexpected effect on him.

Then she pulled back, returning them to reality. Her shock was followed by fear and finally anger. She slapped him, hard, with the palm of her healing hand.

Her eyes were wide. "What was all that about?" she asked as she backed away, one hand protectively across her chest, the other behind her.

"I don't know," he admitted ruefully, "but whatever it was, it's gone."

"I see. Then I don't suppose you'll need this now, will you?" She reached down and pulled the knife from her boot.

"No. I guess I won't."

"Concealing the knife in your bedroll was what this was about, wasn't it? Don't ever try something like that again, Captain Colter, or I'll use the knife on you."

She whirled around, and moments later she was inside the blanket, eyes closed, her entire body trembling like a snow rabbit caught in the gaze of a mountain lion.

She'd known there was nothing out there, but she'd let him play out his plan, wondering how far he'd go. She hadn't expected him to kiss her. But more than that she hadn't expected the blaze of fire that the kiss had ignited, the way her body had reached out, begging to be touched, the way her lips parted, inviting him inside.

"Guess you're not going to take the first watch," he finally said.

"You guessed right, soldier." Her throat was so tight that her words came out in a breathless rush.

"Got to you, did I?" he teased, surprising himself with the lightness of his tone. "The truth is, you got to me, too. But both of us know that nothing can come of it. No two people could ever be more unsuited to each other. It won't happen again."

"You're right, Colter. It won't. As for why I responded, perhaps I have my own ways of distraction."

Her claim was brave, but he didn't believe she'd kissed him intentionally. He didn't even try to analyze the kiss. Giving thought to the combustion only fueled the flame. Best to put it behind them.

"Sweet dreams, madam jailer. I hope you don't have nightmares. I'm unarmed."

Sabrina didn't answer. He was wrong. He had a weapon, a new and powerful one against which she had no defense. He'd started a wildfire and Sabrina felt as if she were burning up.

THE WINDFLOWER

BY

SHARON AND TOM CURTIS

"Sharon and Tom's talent is immense."
—LaVyrle Spencer

With stories rich in passion and filled with humor, bestselling authors Sharon and Tom Curtis have become two of the most beloved romance novelists. Now this extraordinarily talented writing team offers a captivating tale of love and danger on the high seas, as a young woman is kidnapped and taken to an infamous privateering ship and her mysterious, golden-haired captor.

"You're very amusing, you know," he said.

For the first time since she'd left the tavern, she felt an emotion stirring within her that was not terror.

"I wasn't aware that I was being amusing," she said, a terse edge to her voice.

"I never supposed you were aware of it. But don't you think you were being a little overly conscientious? Under the circumstances."

Unfortunately his statement hit uncomfortably close to the truth. Before she could stop herself, Merry bit out, "I suppose *you* think nothing of knocking whole villages to the ground."

"Nothing at all," he said cheerfully.

"And terrorizing innocent women!" she said, a tremble in her voice.

"Yes. Innocent ones," he said, running his palm along her flat stomach, "and not so innocent ones."

She nearly fainted under his touch. "Don't do that," she said, her voice cracking in good earnest.

"Very well," he said, removing his hand. He went back to lean against the porch, resting on the heels of his hands, his long finely muscled legs stretched before him, and gave her an easy smile. "Don't run away from me, little one. For the moment you're much safer here."

Something in her face made him laugh again. "I can see you don't believe it," he continued. "But stay with me nevertheless. If you run off, I'll have to chase you, and I don't think we want to scamper across the beach like a pair of puppies."

She wondered if that meant he wouldn't invest much energy in trying to catch her if she did try to run and if it might not be worth the risk.

Reading her thoughts with alarming precision, he asked good-humoredly, "Do you think you could outrun me?"

It was hardly likely. A man used to safely negotiating the rigging during a high wind would be quick enough to catch her before she could even think of moving, and strong enough to make her very sorry. Involuntarily her gaze dropped to his hard legs, with their smooth, rhythmical blend of healthy muscle.

"Like what you see?" he asked her.

Merry's gaze flew to his, and she blushed and swallowed painfully. In a ludicrously apologetic voice she managed, "I beg your pardon."

"That's quite all right." He reached out his hand and stroked beneath her chin. "Much too conscientious. Would it surprise you to know, my little friend, that having you stare at my legs is the most uplifting thing that's happened to me all day?"

It was not the kind of remark she had remotely conceived a man might make to a woman, but there was something in his matter-of-fact delivery that made her suspect that he had participated in a great many conversations in precisely this style. Wishing she could match the ease of his tone, she said, "It's a pity your days are so dull."

"Oh, yes," he said with a glimmer of amusement, "in between knocking down villages and making people walk the plank, pirates really have very little to do."

Merry wondered briefly how she could ever have been so foolish as to have actually *wished* for an adventure.

"I don't know how you can talk about it like that," she said weakly.

He smiled. "I take it you don't usually flirt with villains."

"I don't flirt with *anyone*," Merry said, getting angry.

"I believe you don't, darling."

For a second his kind, enticing gaze studied her face, and then he looked away to the south, where a tiny flicker began to weave through the rocks. Another star of light appeared, and another, dragon's breath in the night.

"My cohorts," he observed. Offering her a hand, Devon inclined his head toward the dark-blue shadows that crept along the tavern's north side. "Come with me, I'm sure you don't want them to see you."

"*More* pirates?" said Merry hoarsely, watching the lights.

"Six more. Seven, if Reade is sober."

She hesitated, not daring to trust him, her face turned to him with the unconscious appeal of a lost child.

"Come with me," he repeated patiently. "Look at it this way. Better one dreadful pirate than seven. Whatever you're afraid I'll do to you, I can only do it once. *They* can do it seven times. Besides, I'm unarmed. You can frisk me if you want." His arm came around her back, drawing her away from the tavern. Grinning down at her, he said, "As a matter of fact, I wish you would frisk me."

She went with him, her footsteps as passive as a dreamer.

It seemed quite unnecessary to tell him. Nevertheless Merry said, "I've never met anyone like you in my life."

And don't miss these thrilling
romances from Bantam Books,
on sale in November:

ADAM'S FALL
by the *New York Times* bestselling author

Sandra Brown

Now available in paperback!

PURE SIN
by the mistress of erotic historical romance

Susan Johnson

"Susan Johnson is one of the best."
—*Romantic Times*

ON WINGS OF MAGIC
by the nationally bestselling

Kay Hooper

"[Kay Hooper] writes with exceptional beauty and
grace."
—*Romantic Times*

OFFICIAL RULES

To enter the sweepstakes below carefully follow all instructions found elsewhere in this offer.

The **Winners Classic** will award prizes with the following approximate maximum values: 1 Grand Prize: $26,500 (or $25,000 cash alternate); 1 First Prize: $3,000; 5 Second Prizes: $400 each; 35 Third Prizes: $100 each; 1,000 Fourth Prizes: $7.50 each. Total maximum retail value of Winners Classic Sweepstakes is $42,500. Some presentations of this sweepstakes may contain individual entry numbers corresponding to one or more of the aforementioned prize levels. To determine the Winners, individual entry numbers will first be compared with the winning numbers preselected by computer. For winning numbers not returned, prizes will be awarded in random drawings from among all eligible entries received. Prize choices may be offered at various levels. If a winner chooses an automobile prize, all license and registration fees, taxes, destination charges and, other expenses not offered herein are the responsibility of the winner. If a winner chooses a trip, travel must be complete within one year from the time the prize is awarded. Minors must be accompanied by an adult. Travel companion(s) must also sign release of liability. Trips are subject to space and departure availability. Certain black-out dates may apply.

The following applies to the sweepstakes named above:

No purchase necessary. You can also enter the sweepstakes by sending your name and address to: P.O. Box 508, Gibbstown, N.J. 08027. Mail each entry separately. Sweepstakes begins 6/1/93. Entries must be received by 12/30/94. Not responsible for lost, late, damaged, misdirected, illegible or postage due mail. Mechanically reproduced entries are not eligible. All entries become property of the sponsor and will not be returned.

Prize Selection/Validations: Selection of winners will be conducted no later than 5:00 PM on January 28, 1995, by an independent judging organization whose decisions are final. Random drawings will be held at 1211 Avenue of the Americas, New York, N.Y. 10036. Entrants need not be present to win. Odds of winning are determined by total number of entries received. Circulation of this sweepstakes is estimated not to exceed 200 million. All prizes are guaranteed to be awarded and delivered to winners. Winners will be notified by mail and may be required to complete an affidavit of eligibility and release of liability which must be returned within 14 days of date on notification or alternate winners will be selected in a random drawing. Any prize notification letter or any prize returned to a participating sponsor, Bantam Doubleday Dell Publishing Group, Inc., its participating divisions or subsidiaries, or the independent judging organization as undeliverable will be awarded to an alternate winner. Prizes are not transferable. No substitution for prizes except as offered or as may be necessary due to unavailability, in which case a prize of equal or greater value will be awarded. Prizes will be awarded approximately 90 days after the drawing. All taxes are the sole responsibility of the winners. Entry constitutes permission (except where prohibited by law) to use winners' names, hometowns, and likenesses for publicity purposes without further or other compensation. Prizes won by minors will be awarded in the name of parent or legal guardian.

Participation: Sweepstakes open to residents of the United States and Canada, except for the province of Quebec. Sweepstakes sponsored by Bantam Doubleday Dell Publishing Group, Inc., (BDD), 1540 Broadway, New York, NY 10036. Versions of this sweepstakes with different graphics and prize choices will be offered in conjunction with various solicitations or promotions by different subsidiaries and divisions of BDD. Where applicable, winners will have their choice of any prize offered at level won. Employees of BDD, its divisions, subsidiaries, advertising agencies, independent judging organization, and their immediate family members are not eligible.

Canadian residents, in order to win, must first correctly answer a time limited arithmetical skill testing question. Void in Puerto Rico, Quebec and wherever prohibited or restricted by law. Subject to all federal, state, local and provincial laws and regulations. For a list of major prize winners (available after 1/29/95): send a self-addressed, stamped envelope entirely separate from your entry to: Sweepstakes Winners, P.O. Box 517, Gibbstown, NJ 08027. Requests must be received by 12/30/94. DO NOT SEND ANY OTHER CORRESPONDENCE TO THIS P.O. BOX.

Don't miss these fabulous Bantam women's fiction titles

Now on Sale

WANTED *by Patricia Potter*

Bestselling author of *Relentless*

"The healing power of love and the beauty of trust and faith in others shines like a beacon in all of Ms. Potter's work."—Romantic Times

Patricia Potter, winner of *Romantic Times's* Storyteller of the Year Award, triumphs once more with this searing tale of an unyielding lawman and the woman caught between him and his past.

_____56600-8 $5.50/$6.99 in Canada

SCANDAL IN SILVER
by the highly acclaimed Sandra Chastain

"This delightful author has a tremendous talent that places her on a pinnacle reserved for special romance writers."—Affaire de Coeur

In her new *Once Upon A Time Romance,* Sandra Chastain borrows from *Seven Brides for Seven Brothers* for a wonderfully funny and sensual historical romance about five sisters stranded in the Colorado wilderness .

_____56465-X $5.50/$6.99 in Canada

THE WINDFLOWER
by the award-winning Sharon and Tom Curtis

"Sharon and Tom's talent is immense."—LaVyrle Spencer

This extraordinarily talented writing team offers a captivating tale — of love and danger on the high seas, about a young woman who is kidnapped and taken to an infamous privateering ship and her mysterious golden-haired captor.

_____56806-X $4.99/$6.50 in Canada